A MAN OF HONOR
KINGSTON FAMILY SERIES

MIRANDA LIASSON

Entangled Publishing, LLC
2614 South Timberline Road
Suite 109
Fort Collins, CO 80525
Visit our website at www.entangledpublishing.com.

Indulgence is an imprint of Entangled Publishing, LLC.

Edited by Alethea Spiridon
Cover design by Tamara Jarvis
Cover art from Shutterstock

Manufactured in the United States of America

First Edition June 2016

For those who serve.

Chapter One

It wasn't every day that Catherine Kingston found herself in a badly lit parking lot about to beg an exotic dancer to take her place.

The woman—it was hard to tell, but she barely looked twenty if she was a day—stood in the May drizzle, her skimpily clad form outlined in a dim circle of light. Around the top of the lone lamppost, bugs careened and crashed, unable to avoid the magnetism of the bulbs. The woman adjusted the spaghetti-thin straps on her cami and shoved her key into the door of a beat-up Pontiac Sunbird, its fender as crooked as a smashed-in jaw.

Cat didn't have long to collect her courage before the woman would start her car and drive away. For a moment, she chickened out, retreating into the shadows. Where she'd been for most of her life. The neon fish on the STICKY FISH sign blew flashing green bubbles above her and lit the low-lying mist from the lake that wound through the parking lot, giving it an even more eerie look.

Cat had always followed the prescribed road and had

never deviated from it. But she was done being an observer in her own life. She'd lived that way for far too long.

She *would* get over Preston Guthrie. He'd invaded her blood like malaria, a cyclic, rebounding fever she'd suffered with on and off for years. It was time to finally flush him out of her system once and for all.

Whatever it took, that's what she needed to do. No matter how out of character, how scary or crazy. She *had* to move on. Her sanity—and her future—depended on it.

He was her brother's best friend, and she'd had a crush on him forever—one that he'd either never been aware of or had never reciprocated. It had taken years to forget him, but she had. Then, last fall, after her fiancé had dumped her, Preston and she had finally met up again, at a friend's wedding, as that crazy bitch fate would have it, right before he'd been called up from the reserves for a tour of duty in Afghanistan. Their connection, at least for her, had been shocking, charged with more joules than a defibrillator paddle. And just as short-lived, because a few months later he'd dumped her, too. But despite their long history, he'd done it by disappearing without a word.

In the parking lot, the woman's ignition flared, her car a clanking, discombobulated wreck with a bad muffler. It was now or never. Cat stepped forward and thrust two twenties in front of her face. "This is yours for the address those guys in the bar just gave you."

Oh God, what was she doing? It wasn't too late. She could still back down. Walk quickly back into the bar, have a coffee, calm down. Go home. But she couldn't. That time with Preston—it wasn't really *with* him, since most of their relationship had taken place by letters and emails and Skype—had been magical. She thought they'd had something truly special and could have sworn he'd felt it, too. Which was thinking on crack, because apparently he hadn't.

She'd overheard his friends talking in the bar, and this crazy plan had come to her. Preston's friends had apparently decided to send an exotic dancer up to his newly constructed mansion on Lake Watchacatchee, where he was staying while he was in town for Cat's sister's wedding. And since said dancer was right here, within bribing distance, Cat decided to do a little trade. Pay her off, take her place. Which was the height of desperation. Normal people didn't do such things. They had polite, calm conversations with their exes.

But she'd never gotten that conversation. Technically, he wasn't even her ex. Unless phone sex counted. He'd never had the decency to break things off; he'd just…let her go. After his leg injury overseas, he simply stopped communicating. He owed her closure, so she could move on and leave him behind once and for all. Dammit, she owed *herself* closure. For the sake of her own integrity, she would not back down.

The dancer cocked her head to one side, assessing Cat with a wary gaze. What did she think of Cat's silk blouse, black pencil skirt, and pearls, a world away from the girl's dark hair and dark eyes lined with enough liner to compete with a singer from an eighties hair band? Her low-cut top needed pulled up over her cleavage just as much as her skimpy skirt needed scooched down over her ass. In another context, she might've been considered pretty, but now, she just needed covered up.

"You're that Kingston girl, aren't you?" the girl asked.

Whoa, Cat hadn't expected that. She forced herself not to cringe. Being the daughter of the largest employer in town, Kingston Shoes, had always set her apart. Her family had never lived decadently, but she'd never lacked for things. Everything about this girl cried the opposite. She wondered if she'd chosen this job, or if she'd simply had no choice.

"I'm sorry. Do I know you?" Cat asked.

"My mother cleans your grandmother's house. Sometimes

I go with her. I've seen your picture."

Cat was pretty sure she did cringe that time. She bit back an *I'm sorry*. Her grandmother Amelia, or Grandmeel as the family all called her, was an obstinate, demanding perfectionist from the Old South, who still called the Civil War "the War of Northern Aggression." She could only imagine what she was like as an employer.

She forced herself to speak past the virtual wad of cotton in her throat. "Look, I—I know the guy you're going to see. We're old friends. I—want to go in your place. To surprise him, you know?"

A wide grin spread across the woman's thin face. "I get it." She pulled the money from Cat's hand and replaced it with a bar napkin, where an address, blotchy and water-spotted, was scrawled in black pen. Cat didn't need the address, but she did need the girl not to show up there. "This is good," the woman said. "I can be early for my next gig."

"Thanks." Cat wanted to tell her not to go to another bar, to go somewhere where better men were to be found. And if she could figure out where the hell that was, she'd join her there.

Cat waited until the woman drove off, then turned to walk the short way to the grand houses that ran along the lakefront, where Preston had recently built a home. She could have driven, but she didn't want to take the risk of anyone in their small town finding her there. The rain picked up from drizzle to steady May shower, making her regret that decision. She flipped up the hood on her raincoat and walked on.

With each step, her heart hammered faster. She was actually going to do it. Confront him, and finally get the truth out of him about why he had let her go so suddenly. She wasn't doing this impulsive, out-of-character thing because she longed to see Preston Guthrie, even though she hadn't seen him for nearly four months, since just after his injury. Or because she wanted to rage at him for dumping her. Rather, she wanted to eyeball him with a cool, detached demeanor while she heard from his own lips why, in a place where he couldn't run. If he squirmed a little in the process, all the better. All she would have to do is resist his boyish grin, his blue eyes as endless as an infinity pool, and his dangerously hard muscles.

At least she would get all this angst off her chest in time for her sister Maddie's wedding, which was coming up in just a week. Cat was the maid of honor, and Preston, her sister's fiancé's business partner in a venture capital business, was the best man. If they got all their baggage out in the open, maybe they could resolve things so she wouldn't feel like murdering him in front of all the guests and, therefore, ruin the wedding. She needed this closure, for her own sake and for the sake of her sister's special day. At least she would come away knowing why he dumped her.

Then she would finally be over him for good.

• • •

Preston's leg hurt like a son of a bitch. Today had been especially bad, with the plane ride and all the maneuvering he'd had to do, but he'd finally settled in for the night on a cushioned chair in front of the big-screen TV in the living area of his new place, a beer in his hand and a nest of pillows propped under the Velcro brace he wore around his damaged knee. When his buddies had called asking him to join them at Buckleberry Bend's one and only bar, he'd meant it when he'd said no. A cavalcade of raging bulls couldn't make him budge again until bedtime.

He hadn't been back in Buckleberry Bend since before his deployment last September. He'd been flown back to the States after a roadside bomb blew his knee into a thousand pieces in February. He'd endured one round of surgery at Walter Reed, one more a month ago in New York City by a specialist world-renowned for dealing with his particular type of injury. Two down, one more to go.

The house had been finished and then furnished by his staff while he was gone, and this was his first time seeing it. It was beautiful and comfortable, with the finest of everything, but to him, it didn't look lived-in. Before his injury, he dreamed of being here with Cat, of making a home here. It was one of the things that got him through that time. Then everything fell apart.

The doorbell rang at the same time he received a text from the guys.

Sending you **something** to take all your pain away. Enjoy.

What the hell? He prayed the *something* was a pizza.

He flipped open the app on his cell phone that showed him the camera view of the front door area. A woman stood there in a black raincoat and heels. High ones, showing off an expanse of shapely long leg. The raincoat opened at the top to reveal cleavage, a lot or a little, he couldn't tell in the dim light. Her head was covered with a hood, and he couldn't make out her face.

He pushed another button on his phone, called, "Come in," and remotely released the lock.

His friends were out to get him for staying in tonight instead of joining them at the bar. Or they felt sorry for him, for all he'd been through. He liked the first explanation better. Pity was never his style.

He heard the front door open and shut. "Surprise," the woman said in a breathy whisper.

"Well, surprise to you, too," he said, roping his arm around the back of the chair to see her better. He smiled.

Those dumb-fuck friends of his, what or who was this about? But he'd play along. Why the hell not? "Hope you don't mind if I don't get up, sweetheart."

"No need. I know all about you, soldier."

He was certain she didn't. Couldn't know that the searing pain that pierced the flesh of his right leg like lightning rods was nothing compared to what went on inside his head.

So yeah, he'd take the diversion. He hadn't had a woman since…well, since before Cat Kingston had come barreling back into his life, toppling his world like a bunch of bowling pins.

"Aren't you going to invite me in?" The lush tones of her voice held a raw edge of nerves, and something more he couldn't place.

"Aren't you going to take off your hood?" Preston was no fool. After he graduated from West Point, he'd worked in military intelligence until he'd done his time for the Army, and then started a successful venture capital business with his friend Nick. A business now headquartered here in Buckleberry that enabled him to be his own boss and work remotely while he was in between surgeries. For all he knew, his friends had sent a guy masquerading as a woman just for laughs. And if that was the case, the laugh was going to be on them.

"Only when I'm sure you're up for company."

"I'm up for it all right. My leg may not work, but I can assure you everything else does." He nodded toward the chocolate-colored Italian leather couch. "Have a seat." Whoever this woman was, he was certain she was *not* a prostitute. His friends weren't that tacky. No reason he couldn't play along for a bit. Even with his bum leg, he'd had plenty of offers from sympathetic young things pining to do their patriotic duty for a fallen soldier. He'd never been that desperate. Still wasn't. But he'd love a distraction. Love to forget everything for just a few moments: the pain, the hell, the woman he'd left in the dust.

The lady in black sashayed across the room to stand directly behind him, where he couldn't easily turn to see her face. She looped cool hands over his eyes, leaning her elbows on the top of his chair. Raindrops rolled off her jacket and landed on his neck, sending a slight shiver cascading down his back. A clean, delicate fragrance he couldn't quite place enveloped him in a cloud of scent.

"What would you like tonight, soldier?" Her voice was smooth as silk, but her hands trembled, making him think she must be young, inexperienced. She brushed her lips softly along his neck. He would put a stop to this nonsense in a minute, but God, it felt too damn good to be touched.

The image that played before his eyes, stabbing his heart with the same immutable pain as his worthless leg, was of another woman, not vampy, not sultry. Soft blond hair, a smile as sweet as homemade sugar cookies at Christmas. More slender than curvy, but just right for his tastes. There'd been a time before his injury when he'd almost believed he could make up for his shitty upbringing and be the man she needed. But not anymore. And not ever.

The war had changed all that.

That scent. Lavender, that's what it was. Sweet and old-fashioned, a huge contrast to her provocative behavior. *Familiar.* And that voice, too, once you peeled off the layers of that phony lilt.

His heart accelerated, his senses sharpening with suspicion. "Why are you here?" he asked as casually as he could manage while he reached up his hands and curved them around her wrists. Delicate, just like *hers.*

"Your friends sent me to show you a good time," she said. He ran his hands lightly up her arms, stopping just below her elbows.

His heart pumped equal parts dread and anticipation through his body. Too many coincidences had raised his spy sense. Her timidity, the disguise, the sweet smell that had permeated his dreams every bloody night in the hot, arid desert. This was no stripper. Or dancer. Or whatever masquerade she was playing at. He didn't know how or why, but he'd recognize Catherine Kingston if he were blind *and* deaf.

His hands stilled at her elbows. For one moment, he stroked the soft skin, enjoying the forbidden feel of her. Then he tightened his hold, pivoted his shoulders, and sent her tumbling into his lap. The hood tipped back, and he found himself staring into a pair of angry eyes.

"What the—"

She struggled against him, but he didn't ease up. His leg might be just about useless, but everywhere else he was lock-grip strong. He'd pinned her as easily as a judo master's takedown.

"What are you doing here?" he asked. Maybe it was the shock of seeing her, of finally having her in his arms, warm and sweet, after he'd lived through so much, stared death in the eyeballs and spat in its face. Or the fact that he was already turned on by her gentle caresses. In that moment, he didn't give a damn why she was here, only that she was, soft and feminine and smelling as fresh as the lake breeze.

He reached down impulsively and stroked the velvet of her cheek, which was a thousand times softer than he remembered. When he traced a finger across her jawline, the skin of his hand tingled in response. In his dreams, he'd memorized every curve and valley of her face, from her full, soft lips to the delicate arch of her brows, to the light smattering of freckles across her cute little nose. It *hurt* to touch her, because she was his addiction. The bad habit he'd meanly given up, for both their sakes. Yet it now seemed all his hard work was for naught. He could not drag his eyes off of her, and he couldn't stop touching her. She stared right back, her own eyes piercing but unreadable.

He'd meant to blow her cover, outrage her, and send her storming out his door. But life got complicated. Against his own usually iron will, he pushed his hands deep into the silky thickness of her hair and pulled her closer. Her warm, rapid breaths tickled his face. She swallowed hard as her head tilted back, her soft pink lips begging for his touch. Feeling the fine curve of her skull under his hands, he lowered his lips and kissed her.

And oh God, what a kiss. Catherine Kingston's kiss was a lethal weapon, one he'd imagined every day of his dark existence. Now that he started indulging, he couldn't stop.

She parted her lips, more in shock and surprise, and he took full advantage, crushing his own on hers, thrusting in his tongue and plunging deep. For a moment, she went still as the fight in her drained. In one quick movement, she wrapped her arms around his neck and clutched at him, her hands tangling in his hair. Her soft breasts pressed into his chest, her heat penetrating his T-shirt and lighting him on fire. She entwined her tongue recklessly with his, matching each stroke with her own.

The taste of her shocked him, sweet, tinged with wine, as familiar to him as his own shoe size and yet forbidden. Off-limits. He *knew* this, but he was too far gone. Kiss after wet kiss, he devoured her, almost a full year of pent-up desire unleashing in one terrible flood.

Their deadly attraction, one he'd fought for too many years to count, had erupted into a firestorm. He was helpless in the face of it, and too worn down to fight it. She'd found his Achilles' heel, and it was her.

He wanted to tell her everything. Confess that he'd lied to keep her away. Express to her how he'd used her — the memory of her—to fall asleep every night, to blot out the explosions, the cries of his men going down into the biting sand. When the nightmares awakened him, he'd used thoughts of her to calm himself down. She was his Ambien. His narcotic. Only he couldn't ever tell her.

His background, so different from hers, had kept him away from her for years. The war had changed him, inside and out, in ways he could never have fathomed. He'd never be the same man again. And he'd never be the kind of man she deserved, whole and strong, not physically and mentally crippled.

She tugged on his shirt, her hands fluttering over his hot skin like butterfly wings, tracing random paths over the hills and valleys of muscle. Every erotic fantasy she'd starred in over the past year came to life with her tender touch. She was driving him crazy, and all he could think was that he wanted more. In one quick move, he pulled his shirt over his head.

Her water-soaked raincoat hit the floor with a rustle. She wore a pink button-down blouse, the same color as her pretty, flushed skin. He fingered the lowest button, but his hands were trembling. To his amazement, she placed her hands over his and helped him make short work of the task.

He drew back the panels of her blouse like a curtain. Her breasts were small, something he knew she felt self-conscious about, but to him, they were perfect. He traced one with his hand, teased a nipple with his thumb until it hardened through her lacy bra.

One flick and the bra opened, freeing her breasts. He skimmed his hands lightly over them, learning by feel. When he kissed a pink tip, she let out a gasp and arched toward him, shifting her weight. Pain ricocheted through his leg, but he rode it out, more intent on other things. Like the sensations she stirred as her hands roamed freely over his naked torso, how they clenched hard in his hair.

He swirled his tongue over the sensitive tip of her nipple, tugged and pulled. Her breasts were exquisitely sensitive to every touch. The small moan that escaped her told him she was as out of control as he was.

When he looked up, her eyes were closed. She looked like a beautiful, innocent angel, and for a moment, he longed for her to save him, as if that were even possible. That thought brought darker ones, and he silently prayed for focus, to not let his brain mess up the only moment of pure joy he'd felt for a year.

The light from the reading lamp next to his chair played over the carved lines of her cheekbones, highlighting her creamy skin. Skin that begged to be touched. He cradled her cheeks, and that's when he felt it.

Water. Dampness. *Tears.*

Shit. He tore his lips away and jerked his head back.

His disorientation was complicated by the sudden *smack* of the door closing, followed by someone's harsh gasp. Preston looked up to find his best friend standing in the foyer with arms crossed, shock evident in the concrete lines of his face. "What the hell are you doing with my sister?"

Chapter Two

Cat bolted upright, still shaking from Preston's kisses that seared clear through to her soul. She was reeling from the way he'd held and caressed her like she was precious to him. Or maybe it was sheer animal pleasure, and she was mistaken, her internal man compass haywire from too much yearning. She struggled to get up, but his grip tightened instinctively, his big body engulfing hers protectively.

As if that would be enough to protect her from her two-hundred-thirty-pound Army captain brother.

She pulled together the sides of her shirt, fumbling to do up the buttons. How had he gotten them undone so fast? How had he gotten *her* so undone, so much that she'd lost all sense?

"What's going on here?" Derrick addressed his question to Cat.

Cat tried to speak, but lies failed her. The truth was too terrible to admit, which was that she'd fallen completely under his spell, that she'd lost track of time and space, and her body had betrayed her as it always did within ten feet of Preston Guthrie. She sat there, speechless. This was definitely not good.

Preston looked Derrick in the eye. "It's not what you think." Even in the poor light, Preston's tanned face was flushed. She'd never seen him be anything other than calm, even under pressure, and his blatant blush threw her.

Her brother grunted. "It had damn well better not be."

To his credit, Preston didn't try to push her off of him or make rambling excuses. He simply sat with her on his lap, his breathing as calm as if they'd been watching a movie and her brother had just walked in. The dragon tattoo imprinted across his naked chest curled its tail around his left bicep, looking badass and dangerous. The only sign of tension was the tic of a tiny muscle in his jaw.

Coming to her senses, Cat bolted up, folded her arms across her lopsidedly buttoned blouse. "It's all right, Derrick. We were just messing around." She winced. Heat raced into her own face. That was not what she meant. What *did* she mean?

"I take full responsibility," Preston said gallantly.

Cat rolled her eyes. "Pu-lease. I'm a big girl. I'm responsible for my own actions."

"What she means is" — Preston never skipped one beat — "we're dating." Pure shock riveted her to the rustic reclaimed hardwood floor and made her mouth drop open. Once upon a time, she would have begged to hear those words, but now they sounded ridiculous to her own ears.

"What?" Derrick, as predicted, was furious.

Preston turned to her with a wide smile and an adoring look that would have melted her panties on the spot if it weren't for the calculated hardness in his eyes.

"Isn't that right, sweetheart? Truth is, Derrick, I fell hard for her before I left last year and finally realized what a fool I was to have let her go."

Derrick's brows knit into a suspicious vee. "Cat? Is this

some kind of joke?"

Cat cleared her throat. She could think of no reason to play along unless Preston was at risk of bodily harm. Which he was, but really, he totally deserved it. "We were just—"

Preston interrupted. "—waiting to tell everyone the good news. But it's been a long day, and I've still got to do some PT. You'd better go home with your brother, sweetheart."

He was telegraphing her the kind of looks that indicated that something on the scale of a category five hurricane was brewing under his deceptively tranquil surface. Cat weighed her options. She could protest. Tell her brother...what? That she'd come here to get answers but things had spun way out of control? Or she could save her pride and lie, tell him it had been Preston's fault that they'd ended up kissing, and have her brother inflict pain and injury right before Maddie's wedding. Neither choice appealed.

As the maid of honor, Cat felt responsible to ensure everything was perfect for her sister, who meant everything to her. She swallowed the knot in her throat and her integrity and stepped forward to kiss Preston's cheek, where a five-o'clock shadow was already gracing the rigid planes of his dead-serious face. This time, he actually flinched. "Bye, honey," she said in an affectionate tone. But she needn't have bothered. Derrick was already out the door.

The rain had stopped, the only good thing about this night. In the driveway, Derrick opened the passenger door of his pickup with an aggressive tug. He hadn't been this furious since she was fourteen and he'd caught her smoking in the woods behind the high school with her girlfriends.

He blew out a big breath and eyed her dubiously. "Cat, really?"

"Really, what? Preston's your oldest friend. Is it such a crime I would date him?"

"You know I love him. I would kill for him, and I know

he'd do the same for me. But he's commitment-phobic under the best of circumstances. After all he's been through this past year—"

What exactly *had* he been through? He'd been called up from the Reserves to serve, and he'd gone proudly. She knew the leg injury was bad. A bullet had shattered his kneecap and damaged his leg. He'd had two surgeries, and judging from the awkward brace and the way he moved, things still weren't right, if they ever would be. But what had really happened, and why had he shut her out so completely?

Derrick shook his head, still lethally angry. "You were so upset about how things cooled off between you two. I would've killed him myself if he weren't already injured. Now he's back, and suddenly you're starting things up with him again?"

"It's…complicated." Complicated was right. Her fiancé, Robert, had called off their engagement last July, and it had been upsetting. But she'd met up with Preston in September and nothing before had ever felt so natural. They'd simply clicked, and everything that had happened with Preston up to his injury had felt so…right. She'd never questioned that what she felt for him was leaps and bounds over what she'd had with Robert. After all, Preston had felt it, too—or so she thought.

Preston's rejection had totally blindsided her—it had cut to the bone to know he had given her up so easily when she thought they had the possibility of a forever kind of thing. It made her doubt herself. Question her sanity. Think she'd leaped too fast and too blindly after Robert. After her failed engagement, this was just one more thing to demonstrate what a bad judge of character she was. Yet even now Robert seemed like nothing more than a mosquito bite compared to the total body-and-soul devastation wreaked by Hurricane Preston.

"Look, you've had a tough year, too," her brother said. "I don't want to see you hurt again."

Cat bit back the words that would have spilled out had she not pursed her lips tight. She wasn't a fragile child with asthma anymore whom all her older siblings had to protect. She could fight her own battles. She loved her big brother, but she'd had more than enough of his overbearing protectiveness. She was fine, just fine.

Actually, she was lonely as hell. She'd gone to six weddings in the past year. Maddie's would be number seven. It was only a matter of time before the baby showers followed. But still. She could handle this.

Derrick touched her hand as it rested on the seat between them. "He's messed up from combat. Just take it slow, okay?"

She looked at her brother. Big, hulking Derrick, who was such a hard-ass, yet who could carry both his four-year-old twin boys, one under each giant arm, and race around the yard whooping it up like a crazy man. Whose tough-guy eyes softened to the consistency of baby cereal with one look in his pregnant wife, Jenna's, eyes. He'd always been there for Cat and she couldn't tell him to stick it. "I'll be all right. Don't worry about me."

Earlier tonight she'd thought she *was* all right, until those kisses had scattered her common sense and muddled her brain. All the progress she'd made over the past four months getting over Preston had collapsed like a house of cards.

Guilt addled her. She should tell her brother the truth. Confess she'd put herself in a bad situation that had backfired terribly.

Too bad the joke ended up being on her.

. . .

Preston sat on his bed and punched the number into his cell

for the seventh time when Cat finally picked up.

"Took you long enough," he said. He wished he could pace, anything to dispel the excess of nervous energy. He settled for tapping his foot against the floor.

"I'm surprised you still have my number," Cat said drily.

That caught him off guard. Of course he still had her number. As if he'd ever delete it. Just as he would never stop caring for her. "Yeah, well, lucky, I guess." He'd stick to the asshole script. Anything to keep her at a distance for the time they had to be together.

"Why did you tell Derrick we were dating?" Cat asked. "That was the stupidest—" Even as she laid into him, he couldn't help smiling a little. God, he'd missed hearing the sound of her voice. Near-death experiences tended to do that, give you this overwhelming gratefulness for the simplest things. But there was no room for unchecked sentiment, so he tamped it down and did the job he had to do.

"Would you rather I told him you came to seduce me, and things got a little out of hand?"

"I did *not* come to seduce you."

"Funny, because last I remember I was innocently sitting there resting my leg."

"Right before you tackled me and I ended up in your lap."

"I was trying to teach you a lesson." Some lesson. His entire body still thrummed from her touch. He knew that whatever he did now, he couldn't let her think their interlude meant anything, or all his effort in keeping her away the last few months would be for naught.

"Oh, like I'm the one who needs the lesson. Who's accepting exotic dancers in their rooms instead of going out to get laid like normal people?"

"For your information, I don't have problems getting laid. And I don't have sex with strangers. I was playing along for my friends."

She snorted. "You seemed pretty interested to me."

There was the faintest edge of hurt in her voice. He couldn't stand what he'd done to her and was about to again. "I took my pain pills a little early tonight and my behavior was a little—unchecked." *A lie.* He hadn't used pain pills in months. "What's your excuse for that performance?"

"I wanted to take the opportunity to see for myself how you were doing." The line was quiet until he heard her take in a sharp breath. "And to kick your ass about the shitty way you dumped me, you jerk."

Ouch. He deserved that, but he couldn't tell her so. "I was ready to go into combat, and you were getting over being dumped. We both should have known better than to start something last fall." His voice was a dispassionate monotone, even as his heart squeezed so tightly in his chest, he had a hard time taking in enough air.

"That's bullshit, and you know it. We talked every day for months. You sent me *love letters*." She paused before adding, "Which I have, of course, burned."

Whoa. He hadn't expected that. The shy, sweet Cat he knew would never have disagreed so forcefully. He'd have to get meaner, even if it killed him in the process. He did not want to hurt her. But he had to stay strong for her own good.

He made his voice smooth as silk and added a pinch of condescension. "I thought you knew me better than that, Cat. I'm not the settling-down type. I've always loved you like a little sister. It was a mistake for us to try to take that to another level. Besides, you can't dump someone if you don't have a commitment to begin with."

This time, his arrow must have hit the mark, because the line went silent.

"I'm going to tell Derrick the truth," she said. "That I came because I was angry and things got—out of hand."

"Don't do it." He tried to sound firm, but he couldn't keep the pleading out of his voice.

"Give me a reason why."

"I was protecting your reputation."

"Who are you, Sir Galahad? Last I knew, women have been in charge of their own reputations for the past…oh, I don't know, hundred years or so."

"Nothing you can tell him will make up for that visual in his head, of you, his sister, straddling my lap with your shirt undone."

She made a sound between a groan and a wince. "Okay, enough! I was there. No need to rehash."

"Besides, the wedding is a week away. Admitting we don't have feelings for each other but overstepped some boundaries is going to create hard feelings."

"That translates into *my brother will kill you*."

"When you're the one who came on to me. That's fair," he said sarcastically, although she was right, of course. He'd lost control the second he'd pulled her delicious body into his lap.

"Hey, buster. It takes two to tango."

And one moment to mess up one of the best friendships he'd had in his life. Derrick had been his friend since grade school. He'd stuck by Preston through the troubled days of his early teen years. Mr. Kingston had given him his first real job in the Kingston Shoe Store downtown, and Mrs. Kingston, a circuit judge, had kept him out of jail by vouching for him so that he got community service instead of having his ass hauled off to juvie when he'd hot-wired a car at age fourteen. And they'd both helped him fill out the application to West Point. Getting accepted there had taken him away from his abusive father once and for all.

The Kingston family was important to him. Preston was a man of honor. He would work this out.

"Your brother's friendship is important to me."

"That's between you and him. Leave me out of it."

"Honey, you were in it the moment you put that trench coat on and started vamping it up. And let's face it, if Derrick gets upset with you, it will ruin the next week for everyone." He paused a good while. "Remember the cowboy?"

Cat surprised him again by laughing. She remembered Derrick's reaction to their sister Maddie's deadbeat ex-fiancé as clearly as he did. He was a fiercely protective big brother to both his younger sisters. "Derrick drove all night until he caught up with him in Abalone. We never did find out what he did to him."

"Whatever it was, he never showed his face around here again."

Cat sighed. "Look, Preston. I don't want to pretend to date you. And I wouldn't mind if my brother roughed you up a little." He knew her well enough to detect a softening in her voice.

"We'll be at all the same events," he said. "You don't have a date for the wedding, do you?"

"I would rather take my grandmother than have to go with you. Besides, I'm working on getting my own."

"I've heard all about your dating disasters."

"I haven't met someone normal yet," she said defensively.

"I can find you a real man to date." As soon as the words slipped out, he broke out in a sweat. Why the hell had he just said that? This was going from bad to worse. Bad enough he'd have to pretend to date her until the wedding, and worse because he just volunteered to help her do something he wanted to do about as much as he enjoyed eating peas.

"What? You?"

Oh, hell. "I'd venture to say that almost anyone could do a better job of finding you a match than you."

"You know nothing about how I pick boyfriends. Besides, I basically wouldn't even be talking to you right now if it weren't for this wedding."

"Unfortunately, I know a lot because you told me a lot. Let's review. There was the government worker who locked all his valuables in a safe every night before going to bed, and when he got pissed at you, he threw your car keys in there and wouldn't give them back."

"I loved that safe. It was so…secure."

"Then there was the guy with OCD who checked the car locks ten times every time he got behind the wheel."

"He was concerned about my safety. And I didn't mind driving. Really."

"Then there was the thirty-five-year-old who still lived with his mother and loved it because she ironed his shirts every morning and made his lunch."

"I didn't think he'd expect that from me once we started dating."

Preston snorted. "And what about the guy who was afraid to fly? Or the one who kept track of all his calories and cholesterol on his phone and would never eat dessert? Shall I go on?" He spared her the embarrassment of mentioning that pussy Robert, her actuary fiancé, whose job was calculating risk for insurance companies. He spent his spare time doing that in his own life, too—and Cat hadn't beat the odds.

"I'm surprised you even listened."

Oh, he'd listened all right. He'd clung to every word that came out of that gorgeous mouth. During those dark months overseas, she was his lifeline to normalcy. Every goofy tidbit meant he could think of her and the normal problems of everyday life instead of being in hell. He'd wanted to know every fascinating detail about her, and she'd told it all with a self-deprecating humor he loved.

"So I'm averse to risk," she said. "What's wrong with that?"

Part of him wanted to shake her. *You deserve so much*

more. Someone who appreciates every detail about you.
Instead he said, "Being safe gets you nothing. Haven't you
heard the expression 'If you do what you've always done, you
get what you've always got'?"

He heard a creak, as if she were shifting her weight
anxiously. He was getting to her. Good. It was the least he
could do. Help her to see she deserved more than those idiots
who didn't appreciate her.

"What makes you think you've got all the answers, mister?
I don't see you having a great track record on relationships."

"This isn't about me. I've told you from the beginning, I
don't do relationships." He'd never lied to her about that, but
until his injury, she was the first and only woman who'd ever
made him want to try to escape the baggage of his upbringing.
"I match companies with the right people to lead them. In
fact, while I'm here, I'm helping your dad find the next CEO
for Kingston Shoes. Based on qualifications, personality…
it's the same process with the right boyfriend. I'll help you
find the right guy so that after the wedding, you can tell your
brother you've found someone better than me, and both our
problems are solved."

Easy peasy. Even as Preston said it, he mentally smacked
himself. How had he gotten himself into this mess? He was
usually so controlled. He had a will of steel, discipline, and he
almost always did the right thing under duress. Yet he hadn't
been in the same room with her for more than five minutes,
and he'd snapped.

"Look," he said. "I should have been honest with you up
front. Let me try to make it up to you. I want us to go back to
being friends, Cat."

"*You* want to be friends."

"We help each other through the next week, then after
the wedding we go our separate ways. Deal?"

"I don't need your help finding a boyfriend, but if I have to play along, I won't stop you from introducing me to potential candidates. By the way, I'm doing this for Maddie's sake, not for you to save face with my brother."

She sounded as untrusting as a three-year-old on the first day of preschool. Helping her would be a good thing. He'd see her settled, with someone worthy of her, something he could never be. Then he could move on with his life knowing he'd at least done her some good.

Who was he kidding? Staying away from her would have been hard enough. Pretending to date her while pushing her away, even harder. But finding her another guy while he still wanted her so badly—well, that was going to be just plain hell.

He might be able to solve her problems, but his were only beginning.

Chapter Three

"It's too overstimulating in here," Cat said as she balanced on a step stool in the kindergarten classroom and gingerly lifted a square tile from the drop-down ceiling. She tucked in a green string of yarn and replaced the square, then leaned back to admire the bright pink construction paper flower that now twirled there along with fifty others hanging all over the room.

"The kids enjoy seeing all their artwork hanging." Her best friend Finn handed her another paper flower from a large pile on a nearby desk.

"'All' being the key word." Cat looked around the very busy room. "It's not only dangling from the ceiling but also pinned on the bulletin boards and taped on every square inch of the walls. I suppose you would think it was charming. You're the principal. You don't have to be in here all day."

Finn narrowed her eyes and gave Cat an assessing look. "It's not like you to complain about children's artwork."

"I guess I'm just a little nervous," Cat said, adding another string to the collection.

"These kids are little doe-eyed angels. What's not to love? Keep 'em busy, and they'll be fine. "

"They'll sense I don't know a thing about being a teacher. They'll smell fear."

Finn rolled her eyes. "You love kids and crafts and music and everything that goes on in a classroom. What's really bothering you? Don't tell me it's a roomful of five-year-olds you have to keep an eye on for a few hours."

Cat climbed down, heaving a heavy sigh. She couldn't put anything past Finn, didn't know why she even tried. She'd been happy to accept the job of substitute teaching the kindergarten while their teacher was away. Since she'd lost her job as a journalist at the *Philadelphia Inquirer* last fall and moved home, she'd been doing a lot of temp work in Charlotte and for her dad's company. Sick of sitting behind a desk pushing paperwork, she'd put in an application with the school a few months ago and gotten fingerprinted and passed the background check, so she was all set.

In a weird way she was quite excited about it. Watching the kids was definitely not the problem. "Preston is predatory and unpleasant. And annoying. And arrogant." Now she was on a roll. "Despite all that's happened, he's still so damned *impossible.*"

"Honestly, Cat," Finn said, "with a stunt like what you pulled the other night, how could you expect anything else?" Cat felt herself turning redder than the bright cardboard apples, each holding letters of the alphabet that ran in a row across the top of the chalkboard. "Preston did reject you, didn't he?"

Cat remembered the feel of his lips on her mouth, her skin, her *breasts.* As if he'd been memorizing every inch of her, touch by butterfly touch, as his tongue traced a fiery pathway down her skin. Those lips definitely didn't feel like a rejection. "He didn't have to. My brother walked in."

"Um, walked in on what?"

"I might have been straddling his lap kissing him. With my shirt a little undone."

"No way." The pile of paper flowers pitched to the floor, and Finn bent to retrieve them. Cat knelt down to help.

"Preston took full responsibility in front of Derrick. Tried to blame the predicament on himself."

"Hmm. That's chivalrous. Then what happened?"

"He told me he was out of line because of his pain pills."

She raised a discriminating brow. "That's a new one."

"Here's the thing. What if he's been lying all this time? To protect me from himself? My sister says she's seen this in her OB practice—when people go through a traumatic event like losing a baby, they can tend to push the people they love away. Maybe it's like that for him, too. What with his leg and going to war and—"

Finn snorted. She put down the string and the scissors and shook Cat by the shoulders. "You've been reading way too many romance novels. We promised to always tell it like it is to each other, right?" She waited for Cat's cautious nod. "You've got to give him up. He's not interested. You never even slept with him, right? So stop now before you make a fool of yourself."

Cat closed her eyes, letting Finn's words rain down around her like a shower of tacks, hard and pointy and prickly. The truth really sucked.

"Oh, Cat." Pity rang out loud and strong in Finn's voice. "You're so loyal, and you believe the best about everyone. The fact remains, the guy dumped you. He doesn't want to have anything more to do with you. This crazy scheme you two have concocted is just going to be more hell for you to live through."

"I'm over him." No, she wasn't. The other night proved it. "I'm just angry, because I really believed there was something special between us. I could've sworn he felt it, too."

"You're tenacious. And you don't give up easily. Which usually serves you well."

Giving up didn't come easy, probably because she had had to fight so hard for everything as a sickly kid with asthma, which she'd fortunately outgrown.

"Remember Mrs. Hanigan? She never gave you stars for your handwriting. She told you you'd never have nice cursive writing. Remember what you did?"

"Practiced on a whiteboard until I got it. Come on, that was third grade."

"You practiced for *months,* and your handwriting is now beautiful. What about at the *Inquirer*? You didn't make beat reporter, so you did all the human-interest stuff they wanted and more. People cried over the stories you wrote. They donated tons of money to people in need."

"That was all for a good cause."

"And it got you a promotion."

"Which I had for two weeks before being axed with the downsize."

"The point is, most of the time, your perseverance is a great trait, but sometimes it's harmful. You could've dumped Robert long before he dumped you, but you'd gotten engaged and felt bad backing out of a commitment. And I hate to say this, but that crush you had on Preston lasted for *years.*"

Cat looked her best friend in the eye. "That was in high school. This isn't the same."

"Thank God. Remember when you made me come with you to toilet paper his house during football season, and his dad came after us with a shotgun?"

Cat cringed a little. She didn't want to remember the past. "Last fall was different. The emails, the Skype chats…I can't explain it. For the first time, I felt we were really on the same page."

"Could it have just been rebound? You were so lost after Robert left."

"The fact that I said good-bye to Robert is a relief. Preston is more of a—heartache." She caught herself pressing on her chest, as if it actually did hurt deep down inside there.

Finn just stood there, looking at her and slowly shaking her head.

Cat twirled a bright pink-and-green flower she'd just hung and tried to smile. "I'm pretty screwed up, aren't I?"

"You're just lonely. Plus, weird shit happens around weddings. And he's a wounded warrior. You've always had a take-care-of-people complex."

"Have not."

"How many dogs and cats have you rescued in the past five years?"

"Those are wounded animals, not people."

"Be careful, okay? I'd like to see you leave him behind once and for all and find a mature relationship where you're not a caregiver. Hopefully with someone a little risky. Maybe that's what you need, a good old-fashioned fling to help you get your mind off these bad men."

"I could never—"

A knock on the door stopped the discussion. Cat turned to see a familiar face in the clear pane of the door. *Preston's* face. Before she could blink twice, the door opened, and he walked into the classroom.

Cat's pulse ran rampant at the sight of him. The stark black of his suit and his crisp white shirt contrasted sharply with all the primary colors surrounding them. His six-feet-two height dwarfed the tiny tables and chairs. He cut a fine figure, with lean but muscular legs in suit pants that were loose enough to hide his brace, and she barely noticed the shuffle she was coming to recognize as his norm. The clean, powerful lines of his looks were topped off by his close-cropped dark hair, styled in a no-nonsense haircut indicative of a man who had no time or desire to preen over his appearance. Yet another trait she loved.

She. Was. Screwed. Up. Totally.

She tried to focus on all his bad traits. Stubborn, obstinate, *unattainable.* Damn her traitorous body for reacting to a guy who didn't deserve her attention, or desire, or wanting.

"What are you doing here?" Cat blurted. Her face flushed uncomfortably. She was *never* that blunt, or rude. She cleared her throat and gave it another go. "What I mean is, it's a surprise to see you."

Preston set his leather briefcase down on a table and chuckled. "I'm meeting with Finn today about an upcoming talk for the middle schoolers about patriotism. The office told me she was down here." He smiled, a perfectly imperfect smile that made her go weak in the knees.

Finn hugged him. "I'm glad you're back. Thanks for offering to talk with the kids."

Cat shot her friend a traitorous look. Why hadn't she told her?

Preston slowly scanned the classroom, surveying the whole setup, and eyed the artwork in Cat's hand. She wondered if that was how he was in combat, silently sizing everything up like an animal that catches the scent of its prey, then homes in. He focused his stunning blue eyes on her, making her heart stutter under his perusal. "Why are you here?" he asked.

"The kindergarten teacher's daughter just had a baby, and she's visiting her in Ohio for a week. Finn needed a substitute."

"You always liked working with kids."

Yes, she did. But she'd chosen to go into journalism instead of teaching, and she was out of a job. She was helping Finn out this week until she could set up more job interviews besides the one she had in Charlotte on Wednesday. Plus, she needed the money. Plus, her future was a mess, but there was no use bringing any of *that* up.

Finn's cell phone went off. She handed the last of the paper flowers to Cat and took the call. In a minute, she held the phone against her chest. "Your kindergarten assistant, Mrs. McCarthy, just called off. You're on your own today. Are you okay with that?"

No! Absolutely not. Six hours of being preyed on by five-year-olds alone, without help, on her first day? Cat's nerves edged up the scale into full-blown panic zone. "Of course" somehow fumbled out of her stupid, stupid mouth. The one that was somehow smiling, even as she was telling herself over and over to *calm down, calm down.* And *think positive thoughts.* Glancing out the windows, she finally found one. If all else failed, the classroom was on the first floor. She could always escape through the windows.

"You'll do fine," Finn said. "If you have any problems, just push the intercom button."

Cat nodded. "Got it." She would never appear weak in front of Preston even if it killed her, but she had to hold herself back from grabbing at Finn and pleading for reinforcements, any kind. She'd even take the grannies from the lunch line. How was she going to survive a room of twenty-plus rambunctious kids all day when she didn't even know their names?

"I've got to get back to the office," Finn said. "Preston, see you there in a few minutes?"

Preston gave a silent nod as Finn continued her call and left the room. Then he turned to Cat. He silently took the string from her hands, his fingers grazing hers, and easily raised the ceiling panel above their heads. Silently, he finished inserting the rest of the flowers. His nearness discombobulated her, and every touch of his hand sent little electric vibes all through her arm. It also gave her a great view of his lean torso, his strong arms, and his broad shoulders as he reached upward to anchor the flowers. She caught a whiff of his cologne, some manly, exotic scent she'd probably sniffed between the pages of *Cosmo* that signaled *gorgeous hunk of sexy man* and couldn't have been more dead-on as far as she was concerned.

"Need help with anything else?" he asked, his blue-eyed gaze darkening as it flickered over her.

Cat gulped. Not with anything rated PG-13 or under. "I'm good," she said.

"Say, would it be all right to ask you for a lift home…after school?"

"What, your chauffeur taking the day off?" She crossed her arms. She was not letting his hotness get to her. His awful, spectacular hotness. Made even greater by the fact that he was helping her out without even being asked.

"Very funny. My assistant's not getting in until later this week." He nodded toward his briefcase. "I'm going to spend a few hours working across the street at the coffee shop, then I'll stop by, if it's okay with you."

"No problem."

When he reached the door, he turned back and flashed her a smile. "Don't worry. You'll do great today." He sealed the deal by sending her a wink that she felt clear to her toes. And in some other regions north of there.

He left her standing there in the middle of the chaotic, colorful room, wondering if he knew how naturally he'd anticipated her needs and her fears. As easily as taking a string from her hand, or offering a few words of encouragement.

Sadly, that uncanny ability he'd always had to simply "get" her had never translated into knowing how much she'd needed him all those lonely months. No, she was not going to let this strange, untamed chemistry that percolated between them get the better of her.

This was her fatal flaw. She sucked at picking men. Like

this one, who'd dumped her by just disappearing without having the decency to explain why. All she knew was she'd better be careful, because it would be plain stupid to fall for him again.

Chapter Four

Preston hated conducting business in a small-town coffee shop, especially in the Buckleberry Bean, probably because he couldn't get any of his business done. All the old-timers kept coming up to him and telling him how grateful they were that he was back and thanking him for his service. The owner, Bill Colley, kept bringing him fresh refills of his amazing dark roast, and his wife, Caroline, had slipped an extra cinnamon bun on his plate.

He didn't need to be thanked or waited on hand and foot, although he had to admit that their humble thanks touched him. As a kid, he'd been the neglected son of a man who'd never had his shit together, and from a young age, he'd learned to do anything possible to stay the hell away from his own home. It was nice to no longer be pitied for being a hungry, scrappy kid who often volunteered to do chores for money to pay for his next meal.

Giving up on his work for good, he closed his laptop and punched his younger brother's number into his cell. "I'm back in town for Nick's wedding, but I want to see you for your birthday. Twenty-one's a big one. How about we go to dinner?"

The line was silent as his little brother, Jared, thought on that. "Why didn't you tell me Dad's back in rehab?"

Preston paused. He hadn't wanted Jared to know. He'd wanted his baby brother to just be a kid, not to deal with the endless worries that had plagued so much of Preston's own youth. "I was waiting to tell you after your birthday. How did you find out?"

A snort. "He called me—not because of my birthday but because he remembered the cat's alone in the house. He worries more about that stupid animal than he ever did us."

A quick calculation told Preston it had been over a week since his father began his rehab stint, and Dirty Harry, a pure black cat, had been left to fend for himself. "Don't worry. I can take care of the cat." Even though he hated that animal, who hissed and spit and had terrible manners. "Did you send the check to the graduate school at USC? To reserve your spot?"

"Look, about that, Preston—"

Preston swallowed hard. He loved Jared with all his heart, but there were times he'd really rather be his brother instead of his parent. Unfortunately, he felt obligated to be both.

"I'm just not sure I want to go."

Preston bit his lip to avoid saying what he really thought. When he was his brother's age, his course had been laid out. He'd set his goals early and hit them hard so he wouldn't end up like his old man. Now he had to make sure his baby brother did the same.

"I think I might want to work a year. My friend can get me a restaurant job—"

"But you're used to being in school. Why not forge forward and get it over with?"

"I'm not sure if getting a PhD in psych is what I want to do."

Preston forced himself to breathe in and out. His brother was a double major in philosophy and psychology. What kind of job was he going to get without going on to grad school? A vision of Jared sitting on the street in a burlap gown and Birkenstocks with a guitar and a hat for collecting change came to mind. Dammit, why hadn't he insisted Jared get a degree in something more employable?

"Look, let's talk about it when I see you. I'll take care of Harry. So, can you do dinner Saturday night?"

"Um—thanks, Pres. But my friends are taking me out. Maybe later in the week?"

He was a little disappointed. In the back of his mind, he wondered if his brother held a grudge about his emotional distance these past few months. Preston really hadn't told him much about his injury or its aftermath, not wanting to dump his problems on a kid who'd carried more than his share of burdens in his young life. As a result, he hadn't been very available for his brother. "That's fine, but be careful on your birthday. Friends will buy you a lot of shots. You need someone with you so you don't do anything—"

Jared laughed. "Don't worry about me, bro. I've got it covered. I'll talk to you next week. I'll try to make it home next Friday, okay?"

Preston ended the call and stopped a minute to collect himself. Suddenly, he envied Cat. Taking care of a roomful of sweet little five-year-olds seemed like so much more fun than handling the life-altering headaches of a college student.

He didn't know exactly why he decided to walk over to the school a half hour early. Curiosity, perhaps. He wanted to see what Cat was like in teacher mode. Years ago, she'd talked about going into teaching, but her family had nixed it as being too low-paying for a respectable job. Journalism was a revered profession because Cat's grandmother's father, and his father before him, had been newspapermen who had started a string of papers throughout the state.

Preston crossed the main street of town to the grade school. When he got to Cat's classroom, the scene through the open door made him blink in disbelief.

How the formerly tidy classroom could have dissolved into a battlefield of children milling about, construction paper pieces scattered on the floor, and glitter and glue everywhere, he had no idea. Cat sat in one of the tiny chairs right alongside the kids, helping twenty-two kindergartners with their Mother's Day craft, smiling and laughing but also looking a bit frazzled.

Most of the kids were cutting and gluing in their seats, but others roamed about the room. One kid had his hand in the fish tank, and another was stretched out on the heater that ran underneath the windows taking a nap. Two boys chased each other around the perimeter of the room. A little girl was standing on a table with a plastic container of glitter and sprinkling it like fairy dust on another girl's head.

"Joey's got his hand in the fish tank," a little girl tattled.

Cat looked up immediately. A boy Preston assumed was Joey pulled his hand out and looked defensive. "My fingers were full of glue, and I needed to wash them off."

Before Cat could respond, a little girl ran up to Cat crying. "I got glue in my hair."

"My fingers are stuck together," another said.

"Tommy just tried to kiss me."

"I have to go to the bathroom."

That's when Preston stepped into the room and walked directly over to Cat. Bright pink and yellow and green construction paper clung to hair, and she had glitter on her blouse. She was chatting with the kids, praising them for a good job, and trying to field their questions left and right.

On second thought, he'd rather be back in combat than have to manage this tough crowd. He stood in front of the table. She looked up from her low vantage point, her bright green eyes reflecting a bevy of different emotions. Surprise, for suddenly seeing him. Maybe a spark of indignation, directed at him for having the audacity to walk right in uninvited. And relief. All three battled, and the relief won.

"Preston!" She stood up, tiny bits of brightly colored paper fluttering from her lap. She grasped his arm in a semi-desperate grip. "Oh, could you please take Brandon to the bathroom? Because I can't leave and—"

Preston grinned. Couldn't help it, because she looked a sight. Her blouse was untucked. Glue and bits of paper stuck to her fingers. A large chunk of hair had pulled out of her usually tidy ponytail. She'd never looked so beautiful.

Cat narrowed her eyes. "Are you laughing at me?" *Yes*, but not in the way she thought. Even stressed, she was doing her best to direct all these little kids in that kind way of hers. So he bit down on his lip to stop more laughter from escaping.

"You do look a little—"

She lifted one softly curved eyebrow. "Don't you dare say overwhelmed."

"I was going to say busy. And I'm not laughing *at* you." He tugged at a loose curl of hair. It was silky and sprang back at his touch. "I'm laughing because you have glitter on your nose." And it was really cute.

She swatted his hand off. "Listen," she said, lowering her voice. "I'll do anything if you help me out just this once."

He raised a brow. "Anything?"

"Buy you a coffee, give you a ride…"

"Give me a ride?" He gulped. Visions entered his head of taking her up on that offer. But the offer he was thinking of had nothing to do with driving in a car.

"I mean, don't you need someone to take you to PT or something?"

Before he could respond, Brandon danced the pee dance

on one leg, a panicked expression on his face.

"I have a doctor's appointment Wednesday in Charlotte," he said. "Same day as your job interview. Maybe we could go together?"

Cat never got a chance to offer because Brandon hopped over. "Ms. Kingston, I gotta go!"

Preston motioned to the little boy to follow him out the door. "C'mon, buddy, I'll take you to the restroom."

Brandon looked to Cat for permission. "My mommy said not to go anywhere with strange men."

"My mommy said that, too," Cat said, taking his hand. As she passed Preston, she mumbled, "and I sure as hell should have listened to her." She turned to Brandon. "Mr. Guthrie is a friend of mine, and it's okay for him to walk you to the bathroom, okay, sweetheart?"

"C'mon, bud," Preston said, opening the classroom door and motioning for the kid to go. Urgency must have overcome his fear, because he ran into the hall. For a second, Preston glanced at Cat and smiled. He wanted to tell her how adorable she was, but of course he couldn't and besides, she'd hate that adjective. She'd want adjectives like "competent" and "qualified," not "gorgeous" and "sexy" and "hot as hell." To him, she was all those things. Even stressed, she was calm and reassuring to the kids. So unlike his own childhood, where yelling, screaming, and berating were the norm.

By the time he brought the kid back from the restroom, Cat was in the back of the room at the sink washing off someone's gluey fingers.

"Is it time for them to go home yet?" he asked.

"I still have twenty minutes before dismissal."

Preston spotted a guitar propped up against the teacher's desk.

"Do I have your permission to help?"

She frowned. "I don't need your—"

A little girl came up crying, tugging on Cat's blouse.

"Oh, what is it, Tiffany, honey?" Cat asked, wrapping an arm around the little girl's shoulder.

"Tommy just tried to kiss me! And he's chasing me. Make him stop!"

"Tommy! You know the classroom rules."

"They say keep your hands to yourself, not your lips." He made exaggerated fish lips and smacked them together.

"Can't blame a guy for wanting to steal a kiss," Preston said in a low voice.

"No, but I can blame him for breaking the rules," she said with a frown, and he got the feeling she wasn't talking about Tommy. Seizing the opportunity to help her out, he ignored her disapproval and held up the guitar.

"Hey, Ms. Kingston, may I?" he asked.

Cat glance around at the general mayhem. Surrender lit in her eyes as she gave Preston a nod. "Permission granted."

"All right then." Preston turned around to face the kids. "Ten-*hut*!" he saluted and yelled out in a loud, authoritative voice.

The entire room went silent. All action halted.

"Who *are* you?" one girl asked.

"I'm Retired Army Captain Preston Guthrie, and Ms. Kingston is my friend, and I'd hate if anyone gave her a hard time on her very first day."

"She's just a substitute," some little girl said.

Preston homed in on the little rascal. "Hey, do you remember how you felt on your first day of school? Were you a little scared? I bet you even wondered if you'd ever make any friends." He turned to the kids, who were now silent and staring at him. "Now, when someone in the Army yells 'ten-hut,' we stop whatever we're doing and stand at attention, like this." He demonstrated by dropping his arms to his sides and standing up straight, pretending his leg wasn't killing him to do it.

"Um, thank you, Captain," Cat said, suddenly standing beside him, "but I have something to say first. I want to thank you all for being so nice to me today, on my first day. And for being so quiet right now. But before Captain Guthrie plays, I need everyone to line up at the sink to wash their hands. If you finish cleaning up really quickly, we can still have some music before it's time to leave. Okay?"

The kids proved they were capable of lining up and quietly washing their hands. Cat had them sit in a semicircle around him while he pulled out the teacher's chair and sat on it, keeping his bad leg stretched out.

"Let's sing a song." He began to play "Twinkle, Twinkle, Little Star."

"That's boring," Joey said. "Play something better."

"Man, you people are a tough crowd for kindergarten," Preston said. But if he could handle a platoon on the streets of Kabul, he could handle a room of rambunctious five-year-olds.

"How about 'Old MacDonald'?" Cat suggested.

"My brother can play 'Smoke on the Water,'" a girl suggested.

That gave Preston an idea. He began plucking out the chords to "Louie Louie." The kids went crazy. Soon he had them all singing and dancing along to the classic rock hit.

"What happened to your leg?" a little boy asked.

"It got shot at in the war."

"You were in the war?" A little girl's eyes grew wide.

"Yeah, I was."

"Why did you do that?" a kid asked.

"I was fighting for our country. This great country of ours, the United States of America."

He began to strum and sing Lee Greenwood's "God Bless the USA." The kids sat there, quiet and still, thank the

Lord. When he was done, he nodded at Cat. "Is it time to get ready to go home?"

She nodded.

"I think we should tell Ms. Kingston thank you for coming in today to teach us. Who wants her back tomorrow?"

The kids clapped. He sang a few lines from "So Long, Farewell" as a good-bye song that made Cat roll her eyes. He couldn't help grinning at her. She shook her head, but he saw the corners of her mouth turn up a little before she walked away to help one of the kids.

It had taken some work, but he'd finally succeeded in making her smile, and that made him grin even wider. He'd really enjoyed being here with her in this overdecorated classroom with a bunch of wired-up kids. He'd actually had fun. Laughing was something he didn't seem to do much of lately, but with her it had come easy.

So had the desire to kiss her.

One week. That was all he had to survive without touching her. Being a soldier had given him a will of steel. But in her presence, it seemed to bend as softly as a lump of Play-Doh.

• • •

"How do you know all those songs?" Cat asked when the last kid had left and she'd collapsed on one of the tiny chairs near Preston. The day was finally over, and she'd made it through, thanks to him, her archenemy. The man she refused to like. Funny, but he'd been everything she'd once imagined him as being—kind, funny, great with the kids. Too bad he was also a skunk.

He shrugged as he replaced the guitar back in its case. "Guitar relaxes me. I played it a lot overseas and when I was recovering. Besides, you can learn to play anything on YouTube."

"Thank you for helping me. I'm just a little embarrassed it took an ex-army captain to get these kids to settle down."

He snapped the case shut and put it back in place against the teacher's desk. "Still so hard on yourself, aren't you? For being your first day and having no help, I think you did fine."

"I guess it's a steep learning curve. I'm exhausted but… it was good. Really good. They're so sweet, all of them. So excited about being here. I'd do anything to keep that enthusiasm going, you know?"

"Sounds like a calling."

She shrugged. "Not for me. I've already had my chance at an education, and I chose differently. I need to get my butt back out into the real world."

"Looking to settle in Charlotte, where that job is?"

"Now that Maddie's artistic director of the shoe company, she's here for good. Liz is back from Doctors Without Borders and has her OB practice in town, and Derrick lives in Fort Bragg. The job I'm interviewing for has a great salary, and it would be close enough to see my family more often."

"What kind of job is it?"

"It's for the local politics and business beat at the *Charlotte Herald*."

"You don't sound too thrilled."

She hadn't meant to sound less than thrilled, but just saying words like "mayoral debate" or "losses and gains" made her yawn. "A job's a job, right? I mean, a person can be fulfilled in different ways, like through volunteer work and other things."

"You're too young to give up so easily on finding the right job."

She got up and began moving from table to table, sweeping stray paper scraps into a dustpan and then throwing them all into a recycling container. "My family would never approve my going back to school to become a teacher. Grandmeel says, 'Kingstons don't educate children, they educate the world.' Her side of the family has a history of being in the newspaper business, you know."

"Do you always do what your family tells you to?"

With him she hadn't. Preston didn't tick off any of her grandmother's boxes of her finding a husband that came from money and a good family, but Cat had never let that get in her way. "I'm just being practical," she said. "Being twenty-six and living with your parents isn't the best arrangement."

He leaned against the art closet and crossed his arms, watching her with cool blue eyes. "All I'm saying is don't give up on what you really want, even if it takes some work to get there."

Oh, the irony. She had to remind herself he was talking about a job, not himself. Preston Guthrie was a conundrum that could take a person years to figure out. It would be the height of foolishness to continue to batter her head against that wall, handsome and irresistible though it was.

She brought over a bucket of soapy water and handed him a rag, and they began scrubbing down the tables, putting the room to rights. As she dropped her rag into the bucket, their hands touched. He jerked his away fast—too fast. For the flash of a second, a panicked look flooded his eyes, followed quickly by his usual, perfectly controlled mask.

They worked together in silence. Finally Cat tucked each tiny chair back under the tables, then flicked off the classroom lights. "Can't wait to come back and do it all again tomorrow. I hope Mrs. McCarthy will be in to help."

"Congratulations on officially surviving your first day." He smiled at her in such a way that made her feel he meant it sincerely. Like in the old days, when they could talk to each other and they told each other things.

As he walked toward the door where she stood waiting for him to step out so she could lock it, she noticed his shuffle was a little more pronounced than before, and he looked tired. And a little sad. Or maybe she was imagining.

"I want to do more than survive. I want to *nail* this."

He flashed her a look that seemed to signal that all he wanted right now was to nail *her*. Right on one of those low tables with all the colorful paper flowers spinning above their heads. A wall of heat hit her face. How could he act like he was about to flee one moment, yet in another, look at her in a way that dissolved her to molten lava? He was a confident man with a lot of experience with women and the ability to get whatever he wanted. What *was* it that held him back?

For the hundredth time, Cat had the feeling that there was a lot more to his story than what he was telling her. Well, Robert had always told her she'd had one hell of an imagination, and maybe in this case it was working overtime. Conquering the affections of these five-year-olds was going to be difficult but not impossible. Getting over Preston Guthrie and not letting his charm suck her back under his force field, not so easy.

Chapter Five

"Thanks for doing this," Preston said as Cat pulled up to a beat-up, peeled-paint shack of a house on the outskirts of town. He should have hired a driver and gone himself to rescue the abandoned feline. When they were in her car together after school something had possessed him to tell her, and once the cat was out of the bag, so to speak, she'd turned it into a crusade and insisted on driving them here immediately.

He'd run in, scoop up Dirty Harry, and spend the rest of the night watching a ball game, working out, and enjoying a beer on his patio in front of the lake. And not thinking of her.

Cat shot him a worried glance from the driver's seat. "Preston, the house looks worse than ever. Maybe you shouldn't—"

"That's because nobody's home. Keep the car running, and if anyone from this neighborhood pulls a gun, tries to sell you a bag of weed, or flashes you, drive off and go home."

"I have a better idea," Cat said with a devilish look in her eyes. "I'll honk once for a suspicious-looking person, twice if I see a gun, and if the flasher is cute, I'll sit back and enjoy the show."

What was he thinking, bringing her here? He obviously lost all judgment when he got within ten feet of her. "This was a mistake. Let's go back, and I'll find someone else who weighs more than a sack of sugar."

"Preston, it's not that bad of a neighborhood." She gave him a little push so he would get out of the car. "Just go in and get the poor cat."

The neighborhood didn't really give him the creeps. It was all the memories of his father that did. Thank God Vernon Guthrie was well into his rehab stint and wouldn't be here.

His parents had finally divorced when Preston was a young teenager, and he and Jared lived with their mother for a few years. Preston had just graduated from college when his mother died suddenly of a heart ailment. He'd gone into finance and investing with the hope that he would make enough to send Jared to college, pay off his mother's debts, and keep a roof over their heads. By the time Nick and he had started their venture capital business, he'd been doing well enough, and the risks they took paid off in spades. From the time he'd taken responsibility for Jared, they'd never gone back to this hellhole. Although their father continued to pop up at times, always to ask for money.

He thought of the abandoned animal and mumbled a curse under his breath. There was no comfort in knowing his father didn't treat animals any better than he did his own children.

The front door was locked, but he picked it easily with a credit card. One survival skill from his past he could be thankful for. The living room he stepped into looked like an episode of *Hoarders*, with empty beer cans and piles of papers everywhere. An ungodly stench hit his nose, far worse than the smell of greasy fried food and old cigarette smoke. Maybe from the cat being shut in here for more than a week without any care? Fortunately, Harry came bolting out from the kitchen, thin and a little raggedy but meowing loudly. He rubbed around Preston's legs. Preston stooped down to pick up the animal when he heard the voice he dreaded.

"What are you doing here, son?"

Preston startled and accidentally dropped the cat, which skittered away, dammit. An unshaven man with a week's worth of beard, wearing a white sleeveless undershirt and brown pants worn thin at the knees, stood at the junction of the living room and a screened-in porch.

Preston straightened, reminding himself he was six inches taller and at least fifty pounds heavier than his father. "Hello, Vernon. I could ask you the same question."

"Aw, I got tired of those know-it-all rich folks breathing down my neck all the time. I'm just taking a little break, getting things in order, then I'll go back, I promise." His bleary gaze roamed over Preston from head to toe. "How are you? Heard you got your leg shot up over there in Afghanistan."

"I'm doing great." *And thanks for your concern.* "You know that was part of the deal—you promised you'd spend the entire time in rehab." They'd agreed that Preston would pay for the stint in rehab, continued therapy afterward, and whatever else Vernon needed. Vernon's end of the deal was to simply show up, and clearly, that had been too much to ask.

Sometimes he wondered why he even tried with his father. God knows, the man had wreaked enough havoc on their family. Preston had promised his mother on her deathbed that he would try to help him, but so far, three stints in rehab and all the money in the world hadn't managed to buy Vernon salvation.

"Oh, c'mon now, son. You're a powerful man. I figured you could get me some time off for good behavior."

Good behavior for his father tended to last about as long as a TV commercial. Suddenly, it was all too much. The stench, his father's rattly cough, and the beat-up house with all those memories he wanted to keep locked up forever. The longer he stood there, the more they were all clamoring to bust out. Thank God he'd gotten himself and his brother out of here for good. "Well, I was—stopping by to check on the place. I'll be going."

"Say, son, you wouldn't happen to have a couple of bucks I could borrow, would you? Just until my disability check comes in."

Preston reached blindly into his pocket and pulled out his wallet. As a rule, he never carried much cash. As he reached for the fifty he always kept tucked away for emergencies, he couldn't help but see a flash of the photo he placed front and center, one of three he carried with him at all times. One was of his mother. The next one was Jared's high school graduation photo, and the one in the front, of the sexy, smiling woman, was Cat. He ran his thumb over her beautiful face like she was some sort of talisman meant to shield him from this evil. "That's all I've got." He handed his old man the bill, then turned to exit the house.

"Oh, Preston," his father said, beckoning him back.

He stopped but didn't turn around.

"I noticed your checks have stopped coming since I was supposed to be in rehab."

"That's right, but I paid for the rehab program, Vernon. It's one of the finest in the country."

"Pretty hoity-toity it was, too. Kids of celebrities and some washed-up actors pretending to be undercover. All them with their vegan meals and their power smoothies…what a bunch of bullshit. That cookbook guru was there—the one with that fancy cooking show on Food Network. Guess he used his wine for more than just cooking."

Preston calculated that he was around twenty steps from the door. They could end up being the longest twenty steps of his life. "Go back to rehab. They can help you."

"Nothing can help me, son. My problems started with a long-term injury, too, just like what you have. Pills, booze, nothing would numb the pain. You'll see how pain and disability can drag a man down. Make him into something he's not. You'll see how it is."

Like hell he would. Preston clenched his fists to avoid saying anything he'd regret. The doctors at the VA Preston had been transferred to after he'd left DC told him he was their most stubborn patient, as by that time, he'd staunchly refused all pain meds. They'd had no idea why. A blur of black fur crossed his path. Preston made a clumsy dive and scooped the animal up. Over his shoulder, he said, "I'll keep Harry while you're gone."

That meant forever, whether his father went back to rehab or not, but Preston was certain his father wouldn't put up a fight. Hell, he didn't care that he'd left the cat, so he sure wouldn't notice it was gone. Sometimes you could only do so much. Because his father was a hopeless case, but the animal wasn't.

• • •

"Got what I came for," Preston said as he climbed clumsily into Cat's car while trying to hold on to the frightened cat.

"Oh, a kitty!" Cat said, immediately reaching over to get acquainted. She crooned to it and scratched behind its ears and petted its sleek black back. Not only did the thing relax, but it nudged her hand to ask for more. "What's its name?" she asked.

"Harry," Preston said. He decided to drop the "Dirty." At least one of them should have a chance to put their best foot forward with Cat.

"It's scrawny."

"And filthy and neglected. I'm sorry to bring it in your car."

"It's no problem. I have flea medicine at home. And tuna fish. We can stop by."

Preston barely registered her words. He couldn't help looking back at the house, as if he half expected his father to run out and somehow stop him from leaving. "Um, for right now, can I ask you to just drive the hell away from here?"

"Oh, for sure," Cat said cheerily as she sat up and took the wheel, giving the cat one last glance. "She's adorable."

"It's a him. Harry." He took a deep breath, more upset by the interaction with his father than he'd thought, but determined to not tell Cat any of the bad stuff that was rolling around in his head.

"Oh, sorry. You did say that. I guess I was just getting a female vibe. Was *he* your pet growing up?"

Preston snorted. "We didn't have pets."

Cat pulled away from the curb. As soon as she put distance between him and his old man, Preston told himself everything was fine. He willed himself to relax, but his skin was crawling, and he felt a need to take a shower.

"You okay?" she asked after a minute.

He hadn't realized he was tapping his good foot on the floor of the car. "Fine." He was actually surprised when Ms. Enthusiastic didn't barrage him with questions. After a few minutes of silence, he surprised himself by talking. "Actually, not so fine. My father left his rehab program. He's alcoholic and mentally ill, and all the money in the world can't turn him into a decent human being."

Preston was the son who resembled him the most physically, despite their difference in height and bulk. Funny, because Preston had spent his entire life convincing himself he was the polar opposite of everything his father stood for.

Cat pulled into the Kingstons' driveway and shut off the

ignition. She rested her hand on Preston's arm and simply sat there. He took a few more deep breaths, but nothing seemed to help him calm down. Dammit, he'd never meant to seem upset. Must be the damn leg pain, making all his emotions more raw than usual.

"I'm sorry," she said, and he knew by her soft tone of voice and her gentle touch that she meant it 100 percent.

He couldn't look at her. He was too vulnerable, and it would make him stupid, like it did the other night when he'd finally held her in his arms.

"I'll be right back," she said. He managed a nod as he readjusted the cat on his lap.

She returned minutes later with a plastic bag she placed in the backseat. Then she addressed the cat. "You just hit the kitty jackpot, Harry."

"That looks like more than flea medicine," Preston said.

"Just some bowls, a brush, a feather toy, and a collar."

"You're better than a pet store." He turned to Harry. "This *is* your lucky day."

"We take in strays all the time. They wander in from downtown, and my mom usually catches them drinking water from the birdbath."

The thing seemed to calm under Cat's magical touch. It lifted its head to give her better access to stroke along the back of its head, and even settled in on Preston's lap. As they drove the few miles to his house, Preston couldn't help comparing himself to this bedraggled animal, the lucky bastard. He wished it were as easy for him to surrender to her soothing voice, her calming touch. Bask in her clean, wholesome fragrance as he held her close. She was everything good and untouched by the poisonous, life-ruining violence that alcoholism had claimed as its own. Reason number one thousand why any association with him would only bring her down.

After she'd parked in his driveway, Cat walked around to his side of the car and lifted the cat off his lap. Then she held it above her head and looked at its underside. "Well, what do you know." She looked at Preston and grinned.

Preston frowned. "What's wrong?"

"Harry is actually a Harri*et*."

Chapter Six

"You're late," Preston said, sounding more than a little irritated as he paced back and forth near the bottom of his driveway the next morning as Cat pulled up her car. Seeing him with so much nervous energy all the time troubled her.

He'd always been a little hypervigilant, maybe from being a kid whose life was full of the unpredictable, like his father showing up at any time angry or drunk or both, but the war had done something to him. She remembered that during their Skype sessions, he'd be sitting at his makeshift desk in his bunkhouse tapping his pen, drumming his foot so hard that all the odds and ends on his desk would rattle. As if he were trying to hurry time along until he could leave that place. Apparently that habit had followed him home. It was just one way in which the war had changed him.

Cat glanced at her watch. "It's one minute after eight. And good morning to you, too."

"Good morning," he grumbled as he got in the car. He looked a little sheepish, and her heart squeezed a little. He seemed to be trying so hard to be…normal. As if all of it was a supreme effort. "Sorry. I guess I'm a little on edge for the doctor."

"You think?" she said, but she said it with a smile. "Are you expecting some news?"

He sat up straight and stared out the window. "I've been hoping to avoid a third surgery. I've been doing extensive PT, and today I find out if it's working."

Despite her resolve to distance herself, her heart went out to him. She did her best not to think of the way he'd stepped in and helped her with those little kids. Or insisted on saving a scraggly neglected cat. No, better she focus on his ability to push her away. He didn't want her help, and he certainly didn't want a relationship, and she was not going to get drawn into the electric current that was still so palpable between them. Still, he was a wounded soldier, hurting and probably more than a little afraid of what the doctors would say today. It wasn't in her nature not to help. "I have an idea. We've got plenty of time; how about we drive through for a coffee?"

"Well, you do owe me," he said, but she must have looked confused so he elaborated. "You know. You said you'd do *anything* if I took Brandon to the bathroom."

"I'd do more for that than buy you a cup of coffee." Shit. That didn't come out right. Cat felt her face flare with heat. "What I meant was, I'm so grateful for your help that I—"

His gaze flickered over her, starting low with her heels, up her legs to where her skirt had slid up a little over her thigh. It was the look of a man who unabashedly liked what he saw. She swallowed hard. Words failed her.

A slow crocodile grin spread over his face. "I'd certainly take you up on that offer." Did he just— How *dare* he—

He calmly slid on his aviators. "What I mean is, you might have to buy me another cup of coffee tomorrow."

Cat focused on the road. This is what she got for being friendly. He was toying with her. Toying! Just when she vowed to keep her guard up and not even try to make polite small talk, he turned to her and said, "By the way, you look very... nice today." His gaze drifting over her was wolfish, not *nice* at all. "You're going to knock 'em dead in that interview."

Oh, hell. When he said things like that, her steely resolve threatened to melt just like that into a big blob of Jell-O. If things were different, she'd tell him he looked as hot as always, with his navy polo stretched across his broad chest, the tail of that dragon tattoo curling dangerously just below his elbow. The fact that his brace was visible under the bottom of his khaki shorts gave him an edge of humanity that made him even more appealing. He was an intriguing combination of tough and vulnerable, venture capitalist and Army guy, that pushed his sexy quotient through the roof.

She might not be able to control her body's reaction to him, but she sure as hell could control her mind. "Why the briefcase?" she asked, directing herself to safe ground.

"I've got tons of work to do, and I know I'll be waiting for a long time in the doctor's office. Are you sure you're okay spending most of your day with me?"

There was a time when that question would have lit up her world. "My interview will last until one or two. Finn's covering the kindergarten all day, so I'm in no rush to get back. I thought we could maybe meet up for a late lunch and hit a few antique stores to get some ideas for Maddie and Nick's wedding gift before we head back."

"Sounds fun."

She wasn't sure if he was being sarcastic or not. She hated herself for thinking it, but part of her fantasized what it would be like to spend the entire day with him. They'd have lunch at a cute little outdoor café and stroll along the streets holding hands and...

No. This was business. There would be none of that daydreaming that had sustained her during their months apart when they'd both so looked forward to being together. When the anticipation of finally being together, touching each other, making *love* to each other, had been all she wanted and all she thought about. And she'd known that he felt the same.

Trouble was, a good part of her still wanted him. Somehow, she had to squelch that. Remain objective, be friendly, and whatever she did, do *not* cross the line.

She needed coffee more than she'd thought. Cat pulled up to the Bean's drive-thru menu sign.

"Hey, Cat," her friend Sarah's voice came through the speaker, and she waved from the drive-thru window. One benefit of living in a small town—people knew who you were by your car. "Your usual? Tall dark roast?"

"Thanks, Sarah." Cat looked over at Preston. "And for you?"

"I'll have a raspberry white chocolate mocha," he said, leaning over Cat a little to order. "No fun."

She tried to ignore his nearness as she drove up a little in the line, then stared at him. "That is the girliest drink I've ever heard a man order. And what's 'no fun'?"

"First of all, a guy should be allowed to order whatever kind of drink he wants without getting judged. I thought you were a little more open-minded than that, Catherine. And 'no fun' is skinny. You know, no whip, skim milk, that kind of thing."

"The fact that you ordered all that then want it low-fat is a huge disappointment."

"I'm not as active as I'd like to be." He patted his rock-hard stomach. "Have to watch my calories."

"Right, Mr. Washboard Abs. I mean, if you're going to go for it, why not go all the way? It's like someone ordering cake on their birthday and then asking for it to be diet."

"What about you? Don't you ever order anything except plain coffee?"

"I don't ever want anything else. I know what I like."

"You know what you like," he repeated, drumming his fingers against the dashboard. "Or is it more like you're afraid to try anything else?"

"What's that supposed to mean?" Somehow, she had the feeling they weren't talking about coffee anymore.

"I'm talking about your fiancé."

"That's awfully personal." She glanced at the door, fighting a sudden impulse to bolt. Oh, hell, she could take him. She wasn't trying to impress him, and she didn't care what he thought of her.

Mostly.

"Well, maybe I need to know some personal details in order to find you the right match."

"I'd rather not." Yeah, she would really rather not. That was a can of worms she did not want opened.

"The guy was an actuary. His life revolved around predictions. Risk calculations. You couldn't have chosen anyone safer."

"Robert had a great job." In retrospect, that was about all he had going for him. "Why would you criticize it?"

"I'm not talking about the guy's job. I'm talking about his *personality*."

Preston insisted on paying. She passed him his coffee, took a sip of hers, and got back on the road. Yeah, she knew what he was getting at. Robert was as exacting and meticulous in his life as in work. He left no room for spontaneity or fun. Everything came down to ratios of right and wrong. And she'd come up in the red.

She shrugged. "I'm not a risk taker. What's wrong with that?" Preston sipped his coffee, his arm muscles flexing against the sleeves of his shirt. He had big muscles, even bigger than she remembered. She wondered if, since his leg troubles, he was working his arms out double time.

The tail of that dragon tattoo curled around his biceps as he held his cup. She knew now that it spread across his torso, its tail crawling across his shoulders and down his left arm. It was dark and dangerous, just as he was. He'd always been a bad boy. A risk taker to the max. It made no sense that someone like her who never colored outside the lines would be so attracted to someone like him. But she was. Oh my, judging by the way she'd just cranked up the air-conditioning, she certainly was.

He was sitting back, assessing her carefully. "Maybe you are but you just don't know it."

She snorted.

"Taking risks can be very…freeing."

Her knuckles turned ice white on the wheel. His words excited her against her will.

"Life is about more than risks," she said. "It's about faithfulness and staying the course. Those are things that make for a real relationship. But then, you wouldn't know about any of that."

"You're right. I don't come from squeaky-clean genes like you do."

"Don't insult my family."

"I'm not insulting them. I'm only pointing out that someone like me doesn't do long-term relationships. Yet I think I understand enough about people to be of some guidance to you."

"I don't need your guidance."

"Maybe you do, Cat. I think there's a part of you that enjoys risk."

He was such a puzzle, like his drink order. How for months he'd seemed to want her so badly, how sometimes he could still flash her the most smoldering of looks, yet act like there was never anything between them. Like it was all a fantasy she'd made up in her mind.

"All I want is to survive this next week," Cat said. "I promised to play along with dating you, but I really don't need your help finding someone to date. So you can keep your editorials to yourself."

A smart-ass smile curved the corner of his too-full mouth. "All I'm saying is that maybe there's a part of you, deep down inside, that not only wants to play with risk, but craves it."

The way he looked at her, with a slow burn in those Siberian husky eyes, made her shudder. "W-what are you talking about?"

"Or you never would have shown up at my place like you did."

She stared at him openmouthed. His eyes flashed with amusement. She was not about to sit here and take that.

"You may have been a brave soldier, but relationships scare you shitless, don't they? It's a shame, because whatever you're going through might be easier to handle if you let people in."

There, take that. He was so know-it-all, she wanted to shake him. Break through the concrete wall he'd built around his heart. She had no idea if what she'd said had penetrated, because all he did was narrow his eyes and stare at her for a long second.

"I didn't sleep so great last night," he said. "Think I'll close my eyes for a while. Wake me when we get there?"

Maybe. That is, if she didn't decide to abandon him somewhere on the side of the road first.

· · ·

Cat was a half hour early when she pulled into the medical office building's parking lot and turned off the ignition to wait for Preston to be done with his appointments. Her hands were shaky, and she couldn't focus on checking email on her phone.

She was sweating in her suit, and her feet were sticking to the bottoms of her heels.

Calm down, calm down, she told herself. It was only a job interview. One she'd walked out on. One she'd needed. Hell, she needed *any* job at this point. She couldn't afford to be picky, especially when there'd been nothing wrong with the job they were offering. She simply couldn't shake the feeling that she was in the wrong place, leading the wrong life. Everything had felt wrong. Her heart had started racing, and she'd started hyperventilating. Next thing she knew, she'd walked right out of the building and into her car.

She'd never done anything so unprofessional. What if word got back somehow to her family? *Shit, what had she done?*

Restless and hot in the car, her blouse sticking to the skin of her back, she walked into the office building. Preston had said he'd text her when he was finished, but surely he wouldn't mind if she sat in the waiting room. Maybe by the time he came out, she'd calm down.

She walked into a bright, sunny room painted a cool tone of blue with a small tabletop fountain near a window surrounded by plants. That seemed very Zen, so she headed to a nearby seat and flipped mindlessly though a magazine. Her stomach grumbled loudly. She hadn't eaten much breakfast due to her nerves, and it was close to one o'clock. Despite being upset, she was suddenly very hungry.

The receptionist station was shuttered. A door opened and a kindly looking woman holding some paperwork called back the one other person in the waiting room. What kind of office was this with only one patient and a shuttered desk? She wandered up to the counter in front of the receptionist's window and took a business card off a pile. It said *Anita Garandi, M.D., Psychiatry*.

She froze. Preston was seeing a shrink? Oh. Well, she'd

definitely go back out in the car and wait, protect his privacy. Not for the first time, she wondered what was really going on with him. Somehow, she sensed from the beginning that it involved much more than his wounded leg. What the hell had happened to him over there, and was it the reason he'd pushed her away?

Despite her resolve to get over Preston, she felt a faint glimmer of hope. She still couldn't stop indulging the fantasy that he'd pushed her away for reasons that had more to do with what was going on inside him than outside.

There she went again. Dreaming things were different. *Grow up, Cat*, she scolded herself. *Being dumped has made you pathetic*. It seemed, surprisingly, to make her cling even more ferociously to her belief that true love conquers all. But sooner or later, she would have to stop fantasizing about a fairy-tale ending and get on with real life.

Her phone suddenly dinged with a text. *Where are you?* From Preston. She immediately ran to the door and pushed it open. Maybe she could make it back to her car before he saw her.

She ran right into the hard wall of muscle that was his chest. He reflexively placed his hands on her shoulders to steady her, and for just a moment, a desperate desire hit her to stay right there, rest her head against his solid body, feel the comfort of being in his arms like she'd dreamed so many times during the time when he was away. Tell him everything that was on her mind, like they'd done last fall. Tell him how much she'd missed him—missed what they had—and *make* his barriers come down.

For the thousandth time, she had to remind herself that he had thrown their relationship away. Had thrown *her* away. She had to move on for her own self-respect.

"What were you doing in there?" His voice was a low growl.

"Waiting for you. What are you doing out here?"

"I left through the separate exit. You shouldn't have gone in there."

"I—I'm sorry. I was getting sweaty waiting in the car, so I thought I'd come inside." She'd keep the details of her shitty day to herself.

They walked in silence to the car. He limped around to the passenger side and got in, his shoulders set in a rigid line. She started the car and let it idle, let the air-conditioning flood in.

It offered little relief. Cat didn't know what to do. It was too late to pretend that she didn't know what kind of doctor he was seeing. He was a proud man, and he'd always hated to show any sign of weakness. She wondered how hard this must be for him, a strong warrior who thought he was infallible, dealing with his leg injury and God only knew what else.

Yet they'd been close once, not so long ago. He'd confided things about his past to her that he said he'd never told anyone, stories about his abusive father and his difficult childhood. She was not going to sweep this under the rug if there was a chance she could help him.

"Preston, I didn't mean to invade your privacy, but it's not a crime to see a psychiatrist."

He squeezed his eyes shut as though she'd delivered a blow. His jaw was tight, set in stone. "I didn't ask your permission, and I don't need your approval."

His words stung. "I had no idea. Or I never would have—" To her embarrassment, she felt the sting of tears, but she blinked them back. It was just the emotional morning, the constant ache she felt being with him but not ever able to get through. Damn these stupid wedding weeks anyway. Damn their ridiculous deception. Damn her stupid heart for still wanting him so badly.

He sighed heavily. "I'm sorry. I was out of line. You didn't know."

"If you ever need to talk—"

"Please start driving."

He was staring straight ahead. "Okay. I'll drive. But we've known each other for a long time. You don't have to shut me out. You might be surprised at how well I listen. Maybe you need someone to listen."

The car was silent, except for the blowing fan. At that moment, she would have done anything to help him for the sheer reason that he was in pain. But she had no idea how to get through to him. So she put the car in gear and drove away.

Chapter Seven

Preston would have rather swallowed a box of nails than get into the car with Cat. First he'd had to deal with the bad news about his leg. He'd endured two doctors poking and prodding, discussing and planning. The PT was helping, they'd said, although there was no avoiding another surgery if he ever had hope of functioning semi-normally.

Unfortunately, despite all his hours of intensive therapy, he was nowhere near rehabbed enough to even schedule the surgery. A disappointment he didn't want to hear. The word "normal" had never sounded so wonderful or so unreachable.

Then he endured an hour and a half session with a shrink, who'd asked him every personal question under the sun. He'd rather suffer a bleeding wound. That had been painful enough, but all of it paled in comparison to Cat seeing him like this. He felt as defenseless and weak as a baby. He hadn't wanted anyone to know about the psychiatrist. Why her of all people?

He'd snapped at her, and she hadn't deserved that. She'd done nothing but be on his side, and he'd done nothing since last fall but hurt her. They were driving along in silence when her stomach rumbled loudly. "That's loud enough to wake a baby," he finally said.

"We'll be home in an hour," she said in a detached, neutral voice. He couldn't stand to have her feel hurt. None of this was her fault.

In their youth, they'd never really been friends. Derrick was his best friend growing up, and she'd been off-limits as his sister. Not to mention she deserved better than the likes of Preston, who pretended in front of the Kingstons everything was normal despite his home life being something out of a horror movie. Yet, despite a thousand reasons not to get involved with her, there had always been something indefinable between them.

They'd only begun to explore it last fall, before his deployment. Maybe it had been the relief he'd felt at her engagement falling through, but he'd been able to talk to her about anything and everything, unlike any other woman he'd met.

Too bad he'd had to shut the best thing in his life down. He'd had no choice. It wouldn't be fair to drag her into this mess with him. He didn't dare encourage her now, but he couldn't stand to be cruel to her again, either.

"Listen, Cat. I—" Shit, what was he doing? He had to avoid the temptation to explain to her about himself. That would lead to her having sympathy for him, which would make keeping her away even harder. So he stayed on safe ground. "I—never asked you, how'd your interview go?"

"It went fine. Everything's okay." She flashed him a bit of a smile, but he saw through it and her falsely pleasant tone. She'd wanted to help him, yet she kept her own troubles to herself. But he could tell something wasn't right.

"Pull over for a minute."

She shot him a confused look. "Please," he said. They

were approaching a rest stop, so she pulled off the highway and into one of a long line of parking spaces. He got out of the car and put a couple dollar bills into a soda machine and brought back a plastic bottle of Coke, opened it, and handed it to her.

"Have some. Peace offering." He tipped the bottle in her direction. Her cool green gaze looked from him to the Coke. Then she took the bottle.

"You're lucky I'm very thirsty, Guthrie. So I think I'll take you up on that."

He watched her drink the Coke. Watched her pretty lips close around the rim and her slim neck extend as she tipped the bottle back to swallow. He wanted to place his lips on the arc of her neck, feel her soft skin, and inhale her clean, heady scent that reminded him of sunshine and magnolias. She took a few hearty glugs, wiped her mouth with the back of her hand, and handed it back to him. "Thanks," she said, trying to stifle a burp but failing.

He almost smiled, wondering how a soft, girlie thing like her could make a sound like a truck driver belching after a beer. "I'm sorry," he said. "I overreacted. I'm seeing a psychiatrist for some issues I'm having after my injury." *Some issues* was putting it mildly. How about night sweats, nightmares, startling at noises as simple as the lawn mower next door. Not to mention the anger. Hell, he was angry with everyone, especially himself and his effing useless leg most of all. "I wanted to keep it private. My own pride, I guess."

"Just to let you know, I wouldn't tell anyone. Your business is your business." She eyeballed the Coke. "Can I have another sip?"

"I know you wouldn't tell anyone." He hated her knowing how weak he was.

He took a swig himself and passed it to her. Their fingers touched as she took the bottle from him. Such soft, forgiving hands. Such knowing, kind eyes, like an angel. Suddenly, he wanted to get lost in her. Feel her under him, looking at him like that and believing that somehow, the broken pieces of his life would eventually come back together. The need punched his gut so hard, he nearly lost his breath.

"Thank you," was all he could manage.

"For what?" she asked.

"For not being angry with me." He stared into her eyes, hoping she knew he didn't mean sorry for the past sixty seconds, or today, but for all he'd done to her over the past few months. A real apology rose to his lips but faded fast.

It would be wrong to dump all his shit on her. Expect her to save him—because she couldn't. It was a battle he'd have to fight himself. He looked around at families getting out of their cars, headed for the restroom or to walk their dogs on the dog paths. He wondered where they were going. Judging by the carriers atop the car roofs, most of them were on a spring vacation. Forgetting their worries and problems. Lucky them.

"Don't mention it." Her stomach grumbled again.

"There's a nice little restaurant about fifteen minutes up the road. Want to stop and get some lunch? Then you can tell me how your interview *really* went."

She looked surprised. "What makes you think it didn't go well?"

He shrugged. "Just a gut feeling." He had a lot of those with her. Maybe it was something as simple as knowing what it meant when she worried her lip or crinkled her forehead up when she had something on her mind. "Besides, didn't you say you wanted to check out an antique store or two for a wedding gift?" Her face lit up. He hated all forms of shopping, but by God, he'd suffer through it if it made her forget her own troubles.

She flashed a beautiful grin and handed him back the Coke. "I thought you'd never ask."

• • •

"How do you know this place?" Cat asked as they sat down at an umbrella-covered table shaded from the hot May afternoon sun. They were at a sidewalk café on the main street, which was lined with quaint shops. Containers of bright red geraniums hung in rectangular boxes along the white iron fence that separated the seating area from the sidewalk.

"I know this place because it's got the best burgers in the state." Preston looked up from the menu. "You aren't vegetarian, are you?"

Cat shook her head. "I'd love a burger."

"Want an appetizer?"

"I'm fine, thanks." Actually, her stomach disagreed— loudly—but she didn't want to make a fuss about feeling starved.

"Okay." Preston summoned a waiter, a young guy of college age, who was happy to take their drink and appetizer orders. Preston held up the menu and pointed to things as he talked. "Can we please have an order of your mushroom bruschetta and some of this cheese dip and—what would you like to drink, Cat?"

Cat hesitated as he read off half the appetizer menu. "Water's fine."

"Okay. We'll have two waters and two piña coladas. Thanks." He ordered quickly and with authority.

She leaned over and asked in a quiet voice, "We're drinking at lunch?"

"You look like you could use a drink. You still like piña coladas, don't you?"

She *loved* piña coladas. She wasn't sure which surprised her more—the fact that he remembered her favorite drink or that he knew she needed one.

After the crappy day she was having, she wasn't foolish

enough to nurse the illusion of being a couple, sitting together outside on a warm spring day, no matter how tempting that was. Truthfully, right now she could sure use a friend along with that drink.

She pretended to read the menu, but she already knew she wanted the biggest-ass cheeseburger on it. That gave her plenty of time to assess him over the top. The irony stung—to be sitting in a quaint restaurant with a man who knew her so well yet wanted nothing—romantically, anyway—to do with her.

She wasn't the kind of woman to hold his interest. He was a player who'd never committed to any woman. Why had she expected it would be any different with her?

She studied him studying his menu. There was a heaviness that remained over him like a cloud. A crease in his brow, more lines around his eyes, maybe from the physical pain, but she imagined it was from a whole lot more. The more she spent time with him, the more she saw the exhausting weight that seemed to pull at him from the inside. If she could help him clear his inner burdens away, would he want her? Finn and Cat's sisters would call her a fool, but a sense that pricked at her from deep in her gut wouldn't quit. Breaking through to this stubborn, powerful man would not be an easy task, but what if she dared to try?

"How do you like your burger?" she asked out of the blue.

"I'm an everything kind of guy."

"There's no topping you don't like?"

"I like all of it, all kinds of ways. Depends on my mood. How about you?"

Cat gulped. Discussing burgers was not sexual. So why was that all she could think about? Also how could she admit to him that the only way she ever ate them was *plain*? "I—I guess I'm tired of same-old, same-old."

"Another reason you need me to find you a better

boyfriend. Maybe it's time you tried some new experiences."

Wow, it was getting really warm out here. She used the menu to fan herself.

Their drinks and appetizers arrived. He didn't hesitate to pluck out a piece of cheesy, mushroom-covered bruschetta and place it on her plate. "So what happened at the job interview?" he asked.

She rotated the menu uneasily against the white tabletop. "I walked out."

He laughed. A loud, weird, *real* laugh she hadn't heard in a long time.

She swatted at him with the menu. "Not funny."

He put his hands over hers, forcing her to stop playing with the menu. His touch was supposed to be comforting, but it wasn't. It was *electrifying.* She found it hard to focus on his words. "Oh, come on," he said, his mouth turning up in a grin. "It is a little funny. You're the most by-the-book person I know. This is completely out of character."

He wasn't pulling his hands away. Tingles were zipping up her arm and traveling to other, farther-away parts. It was getting hard to converse, let alone breathe. "It's not that out of character. I mean, I did lend Maddie five thousand dollars out of my honeymoon account to buy Nick in a bachelor auction. So I do have my moments."

His hands were big and warm over hers. They felt so good. Wait, what was she doing? She pulled her hands away. He was saying something she wasn't following at all. "Um, what did you say?"

"I asked why you did it. Left your interview."

She tucked her hands in her lap where they'd be safe. "I suppose that's another one of my faults. I tend to believe my gut feelings. Sometimes that gets me in big trouble." Like now, she was suddenly very aware of his deep blue gaze focused on her and only her. For a moment, their gazes locked. That sent a wash of heat cascading into her face. Every cell in her body went on full alert.

He broke the staring contest and cleared his throat. Could this get any more awkward? "What was off about it?" he asked.

"That's the thing, Preston. Everyone was friendly. Welcoming, even. They appreciated my experience from Philadelphia. There were equal numbers of women on the committee as well as men. And their paper isn't in jeopardy of being cut down in size."

"But?"

"But I wasn't…feeling it. I mean, maybe I should say I *was* feeling it, in a long-term way. I envisioned myself at forty, sitting behind my desk with my potted plant, rushing to get my copy done for the day." She paused, looking a little sad. "I didn't like that image of myself. For no other reason than it feels like it doesn't fit. Does that make any sense?"

He let out a soft exhale. His face looked pained, as if something she'd said had struck him. "There are times we see visions of ourselves that aren't who we really are." He glanced down at his leg.

"How did it happen?" she asked softly.

Their burgers arrived then, saving him from answering. He dumped a load of ketchup on his already-loaded burger and took a bite. At least now she knew how he liked his burger.

"It's okay," she said, ready to dig into her own. "We can change the subject."

He put down the burger and wiped his mouth with his napkin. "I took a bullet for one of my squadron mates. I jumped in instinctively, but I wasn't quite fast enough to get us both out of the way. It caught me in the leg and shattered my knee."

"What about your buddy?"

"He and his wife just had a baby girl."

Her eyes began to tear up suddenly.

He shifted in his seat. "Oh, come on now, don't cry."

"I'm not crying." She swiped at the corners of her eyes.

"I bet you cry at sappy old movies. And weddings."

"Don't forget baptisms, baby showers, and bar mitzvahs, too."

"Well then, get ready to open the floodgates. Want to know the best part?"

"What's that?"

"They asked me to be godfather." Then the smart-ass handed over his napkin.

She used it to daub at her eyes even as she rolled them at him. He sat across from her and chuckled.

"You're a hero," she said. "Whatever bad feelings you have about the war, at least you know you did a good thing. A really good thing."

"It's not the people you helped that gets you. It's the ones you couldn't save."

Their gazes caught again across the tiny table. He had the most expressive blue eyes. The same color as the spring sky behind him, and so full of feeling. Cat could not imagine what he had gone through in combat. She wished she could say something, anything funny to bring the laughter back into them, but words escaped her.

"I was doing my job," he said in a detached tone. "And speaking of doing my job, I found you a prospect. To date." He pulled out an iPad from his briefcase. "An investment banker. I've known him a long time. I can vouch for the fact that he's a great guy."

"Oh, wonderful." She rubbed her hands together in faux excitement, but deep down, she didn't have the heart for it.

The man on the screen was white-haired. Not gray on the sides or even gray all over but as stark white as a bleached sheet flapping in the breeze.

"I've known Carlos since I graduated from college."

"Is he your grandfather?"

"Ha ha. Very funny."

"Has he been married?"

"He's a widower. He's fifty-three."

"Kids?"

"Five."

She shut the iPad. "This does not count as a genuine prospect."

"I can't help it if you shallowly reject good candidates based solely on their appearance."

"I am not shallow."

He shrugged. "I don't know what else I would call it."

"I'm not attracted to fifty-three-year-olds. And he doesn't even look fifty-three. He looks *seventy*-three."

"Your problem, not mine."

"You suck at this!"

"Maybe you can help me narrow my search by telling me what you're looking for in a guy."

"Kind, ambitious, cute. Not a grandfather. Someone who loves me just the way I am."

"Who *wouldn't* love you the way you are?"

For a second, her heart sped up before she reminded herself he was being polite and friendly. Plus, he was busy attacking his burger. "Robert was always trying to change me. Telling me to be more outgoing. Or more frugal. To sit up straighter." She took a sip of her drink. "To get breast implants."

Preston choked on his burger, then took a quick sip of his drink. "That bastard."

Heat flooded her face. His reaction was swift and merciless, and it pleased her to her core. "I kept thinking it was all the job stress he was under. I made allowances, but looking back, I was only making excuses. Maybe I thought

I could settle for unexciting and comfortable because it was easier than starting over."

"You're perfect just the way you are," Preston said, "and one day some man is going to realize that, Cat. Until then, don't you dare settle for anyone less."

His eyes sparked with conviction. Emotions flickered across his face that she couldn't interpret—regret, anger, and something else much darker. *Want.* She could swear he looked at her the way a man looks at a woman he wants to kiss, long and hard and deep.

Her man compass was haywire, she couldn't let herself forget. Robert had done a number on her, and she didn't trust herself anymore. Didn't trust what she knew and what she didn't. It was that damn imagination of hers again, wanting to whisk her off to fantasyland when she needed to stay fully tethered to earth.

Maybe his comments had stirred her. Or maybe the piña colada had made her talky. "I'm not perfect. I'm a people pleaser. I had an opportunity to take my honeymoon ticket and go to Hawaii alone, but I didn't. Do you know why?"

He stopped eating and looked at her. "Why didn't you?"

"It seemed too...extravagant. I felt bad. Like people would think...I was sticking it to him by going by myself, so I canceled everything and gave him half the money back. But I should have gone, if only to get the hell away from everyone who thought he was the perfect man for me, because he wasn't. Not at all. So next time I break an engagement, I'm definitely doing what I want and not listening to what everyone else *thinks* I want."

"You should have gone without the bastard to Hawaii. Did you at least use your half of the money?"

She shrugged. "Kind of." What she did with the money was private. She hadn't told anyone except her family.

His thick brows raised in curiosity. "What'd you use it

for?"

"Oh, just forget it." She waved her hand dismissively. "Nothing, really."

"Come on. Tell me."

"Okay, fine. A few weeks later I flew to Vegas, stayed at the Bellagio, and bought front-row tickets for Celine Dion."

"Wow. Risky." He shook his head, grinning. Like it wouldn't have been his first wild choice for sure. "Did you go by yourself?"

"Yep." Cat didn't care what he thought. "I saw her show three nights in a row. It was *fabulous*."

Preston laughed, pretty heartily. It created little crinkles around his eyes that were very, very appealing. "Look, you did what you wanted about Celine, and it was right for you. Don't worry about the interview today. Your gut was telling you something important, and you listened to it."

Right. If she listened to what her gut was telling her about him, she'd have tackled him before their food arrived and they'd both have ended up under the table. How would that be for risky?

Before she could respond, the dessert menu arrived.

"Speaking of living dangerously, want to split a sundae?" she asked.

"I'm watching my figure," he said, patting his washboard abs again.

"Oh, c'mon, soldier. Have some fun. It's only ice cream."

"Fine. You order."

"Is there any kind of ice cream you don't like?" she asked.

His mouth turned up into a slow grin. "I like it all," he said, his eyes roving up and down her body. She felt her cheeks heat again, and she pretended to concentrate on the menu. What was it about him and talking about food that got her so aroused?

"You're certainly easy to please," Cat said. Robert

wasn't, and she'd often blamed herself for not living up to his expectations. It had taken her too long to realize he'd demanded unreasonable things.

Preston excused himself to go to the restroom, and Cat ordered a sundae with four different flavors of ice cream topped with hot fudge and caramel sauce. She felt a little reckless and dangerous. Besides, after that cheeseburger, who was even counting calories anymore?

As soon as he returned to their table, she reached over and put a hand over his eyes.

"What are you doing?" The hard planes of his face shifted under her hands, and she fought a sudden urge to trace down his solid cheekbones, cup his beautiful face between her palms.

She wasn't really sure what she was doing, but it was too late not to go with it. She lifted her hand away. "I'm going to have you taste a flavor of ice cream, and I want you to guess what it is."

"Seriously?"

"Yeah. Seriously. Your body language is telling me you want to have more fun. Unless the war did something to your taste buds?"

The sultry look that swept her up and down signaled that his idea of fun probably wasn't related to ice cream. "Only made them appreciate the finer things more." He full-out grinned. Then he closed his eyes, folded his arms, and rested them on the table. "For the record, you're the one who thinks I need to have more fun, but okay. Hit me."

"Here comes round one." She placed some ice cream on her spoon and held it up to his lips. To make sure he wouldn't cheat, she covered his eyes again. "Name the flavor."

"Mint chocolate chip. This is too easy."

"How about this one?"

"Butter pecan."

"And this?"

"Strawberry. Why on earth would you mix all these flavors together in one bowl?"

"Hey, you're the one who likes the raspberry white chocolate mochas. Variety is the spice of life. Last one."

The spoon hovered over his full lips, sinful lips that she could imagine sliding over her naked skin far too easily. She took a breath and tried to compose herself, tried to stop the current between them from escalating to shock levels. She sensibly started to remove her hand from his eyes, but he seized her wrist with his hand and lowered it down slowly. Then he opened his eyes and looked straight at her with his bright, intense gaze. "Chocolate," he said. "It's chocolate. My favorite."

His grasp was strong yet gentle. There went those big hands with beautiful long fingers, touching her again, sending heat and fireworks bursting everywhere.

No more touching. It was effing with her body *and* her mind. God, she'd missed this back-and-forth, this repartee that came to them so easily. She couldn't help feeling what else would be so natural between them.

Making love would. She *felt* it, down to her bones.

His eyes were blue and troubled, like a raging ocean. She suddenly wanted to replace the ice cream with her lips. Kiss him until he forgot whatever it was that tormented him.

A sensible voice inside her reminded her to *be careful*. She tugged at her hand, but he held it firmly. She opened her mouth to protest, but he stunned her by kissing the inside of her wrist. He surely must have felt her pulse skitter as he pressed his lips against the thin, sensitive skin. "I know what you're trying to do," he said. "Divert me from my problems. You've always had a thing for wounded animals, but I'm not a rescue puppy. Go find someone else, a nice guy who hasn't had to see and do the things I have. Someone who's a hell of a lot less trouble."

"Like Grandpa?" Her eyes gestured toward the iPad.

His fine, full mouth turned up just a little. She struggled to read him, but it was impossible. At times, his eyes seemed an icy blue, like he was trying so hard to look unaffected and distant, but then the ice would thaw, and some warmth would seep through, like embers from a fire barely kept alive.

Something *was* alive in there. She just knew it. But she would be a fool to try to coax it out. She was done playing the fool, no matter how hot Preston Guthrie was or how intensely her traitorous body wanted him.

All Cat knew was she had to get away from him, because all her resolve was beginning to melt just like the ice cream on their sundae.

Chapter Eight

Something had changed over lunch. Cat had gotten to him, worked her sweet, stealthy way under his skin until he was burning for her. He had to try harder to distance himself. Kissing her wrist was an impulsive mistake, but it was a simple blunder, one that wouldn't create any lasting damage as long as he didn't repeat it. If only this damn afternoon would end.

"Why do you hate antiques so much?" Cat asked as Preston held open the door of the first of a string of antique shops on the main drag of town.

A large lamp in the front window caught his attention, and he couldn't help but look. At its base was a haughty and proud rooster, its beak up in the air, wings poised to flap, as if he were about to strut around the barnyard and show everyone how amazing he was. To make matters worse, there was a chicken lamp, too, and together they were quite a pair. Cat saw Preston pause and stopped to see what he was staring at. "I just don't like old stuff," he said.

That was an understatement. Everything about his growing up was old, beat-up, and out of whack, from their shabby house to their barely-running cars to the years of hand-me-down clothing he wore with embarrassment. He'd taught himself to sew just so he could repair the holes and tears.

Cat whistled. "Those are some amazing lamps."

She sounded dead serious, which made him shake his head in disbelief.

A bell tinkled as they entered the shop, which was filled with objects crammed into every available spot. Sections were split into rows of stalls for the separate antiques vendors who ran them. The smell of—how else could he describe it but of *old stuff*; dust, old paper, and mildewed book pages—permeated the place and made him want to sneeze.

Cat picked up an old wide-brimmed hat with aqua sequins and feathers and put it on her head, puckering her lips and making a face. "Old stuff is fun. It's memories of childhood. A peek into how everyday life was in the decades before we were born."

"You shouldn't try that thing on," Preston said, removing the hat from her head and putting it back on a hat stand.

"Why not?" she asked.

"It might have lice or something," he said.

Cat moved on to a stall loaded with porcelain china plates imprinted with all types of dainty floral patterns. She picked up one lined with pink roses and examined it. "For the risk taker that you are, you certainly seem overprotective."

"Only with people I—like. Only with people I like." Oh, hell. What was the matter with him? He'd almost slipped up big-time. This place was making his skin crawl, and he couldn't wait to get out, if only he could marshal Cat away from exploring every dish, book, knickknack, and tchotchke she laid eyes on. He found her at the back of a stall admiring crystal stemware with a finely engraved, etched pattern.

"You like that stuff?" he asked.

"It's pretty and unique. I like quirky stuff. Like, I want to have all kinds of plates one day, and mix them up as a set. I don't like matchy-matchy stuff." She picked up a plate rimmed with delicate painted flowers and another with a traditional blue-and-white Chinese pattern.

"You like to mix it up, huh?" He was just the opposite. He'd take order and symmetry any day over chaos. If anyone said that was because of his childhood, they were damn right.

She shrugged. "I suppose it's because my grandmother has always been such a stickler about etiquette. And china patterns and silverware and glassware. Did you know she started a hope chest for me when I was six?"

"What's a hope chest?"

"A place to store linens and china and serving ware—stuff you need when you get married."

"That sounds kind of nice to me." That someone cared enough to help you with your future was something he'd had no experience with.

"It wasn't motivated by *nice*. It was motivated by her wanting me to follow in her footsteps. Her gifts are conditional. I don't want her stuff or her rules."

Cat's adamant tone and the edge in her voice surprised him for someone usually so calm and assuaging. Preston had had a few glimpses of Amelia Kingston from his youth, when he grew up with Derrick. From what Nick had told him, she was still a real pill, possessing impossibly high expectations and love that was given or withdrawn based on whether or not they were fulfilled.

"It was her idea for me to interview for that job in Charlotte."

Preston picked up a feathered red-and-black sequined mask on a stick and held it up to his eyes. "Tell me how you really feel about that," he said.

She laughed, but then her smile dissolved. "I need a job, so I guess an interview is a good thing, isn't it?" Then she moved on to the next stall, which featured delicate old glass Christmas ornaments with tiny propellers that spun in the breeze and a giant collection of ceramic roosters of all different sizes.

"What do you think about these for a wedding gift?" He pointed to a pair of silver candlesticks locked in a glass case. Everyone bought candlesticks for newly married couples, didn't they? As Cat walked over, a saleswoman with gray hair and a print blouse walked over to the case, unlocked it, and set out one of the candlesticks on a blue velvet cloth.

"These are sterling silver candlesticks, exactly like a pair made for King Louis XIV in the early 1700s," she said.

"They're very fancy," Cat said.

"Notice the scrollwork and the animal heads etched into them," the woman continued. "And there's a coat of arms engraved at the base."

Preston turned the candlestick over to study the underside of the base. "If it were real, it would have the warden's mark here."

"What's a warden's mark?" Cat asked.

"It's a stamp that indicates it contains just the right amount of silver. Silversmiths had to add a certain amount of copper, because silver is too soft to mold into anything."

"That's interesting," Cat said.

"He's right," the woman said. "Silver on its own is valuable, but it needs a bit of copper to really make something of itself."

"How much are they?" Cat asked.

"Three hundred," the woman said.

"Thanks for showing them to us." Preston steered Cat across the aisle. "We'll think about it."

"You didn't like them?" Cat asked. "Too expensive?"

He laughed. "They were imitations."

"And that's too much money to pay for imitations?"

"No. What I'm saying is, why buy imitations when you can

get the real thing?"

"So are you planning a Louvre break-in anytime soon? Or are you just going to buy a pair for ten grand at Christie's?"

He flashed a smile. "Neither. Let's just keep searching for more ideas."

"How did you know that stuff, anyway?"

He shrugged. "History's a hobby of mine," he said, enjoying the feel of her arm as he led her across the way.

"Oh, look at these," Cat said, looking at a giant ceramic rooster with a multicolored plume of tail feathers surrounded by smaller roosters in different sizes and colors. "Beautiful."

"I'm getting the feeling you have a thing for roosters," he said. "Don't tell me. Quirky."

"You're getting me. You're really getting me," she said with a grin.

He picked up a shiny steel sword that was around four feet long, and held it straight up in the air. Looking from the blade to her, he asked, "You love roosters?"

"Yes! The way they strut around showing off their feathers, like they don't have a care in the world." She moved down the line. "Look, a husband and wife." She picked up a pair of salt and pepper shakers, a hen and a rooster, in vibrant greens, reds, and yellows. "I love these!"

He put down the sword and picked up the shakers from her hands. "Hey! What are you doing with my chickens?"

"I want to get these for you."

"Preston, no! I'm just fooling around. I don't even have a place to put them. I'm living in my old bedroom, remember?"

He examined the pair. "You need these chickens." She giggled and tried to take them from him, but he held on tight. When she laughed, her sea green eyes danced and he'd have given his entire right leg right then just to kiss her. Not to mention all the other things he wanted to do to her. "Listen. You need to put these by your bed, and when you look at them, I want you to think of having your own place again and shaking them onto your eggs every morning to remind yourself to turn things upside down a bit. What is life if you don't rock the boat a little?"

She stopped laughing. The tug-of-war between them had ended, and now their hands were stock-still, fingers locked together around the ceramic chickens. "Don't let anyone break your spirit, Cat. Or tell you that you should be a certain thing or a certain way. You'll find yourself if you listen to what's in here, not to the voices outside your own head." He tapped on her upper chest. Her eyes grew big and wide as they stared into his. He'd never seen such a beautiful woman, both inside and out. So beautiful, his chest ached. His heart felt like a wrung-out rag, dried out and desperate from these months of continual wanting and not having.

"May I help you?" an older woman wearing a checkered apron said.

"Yes," Cat said. "We'll take these," she said, handing over the shakers. "And this." She bent to pick up the sword.

"Oh, no you don't," he said, but she'd already laid it out on the counter. "Are you crazy?"

"This is a replica of Excalibur," the woman said. "Notice the medieval designs on the blade, and the dragons and beasts on the guard and pommel."

Cat turned to him and said softly, so that only he could hear, "You want me to shake it up, and I want you to slay your dragons."

She took out her credit card, but before she could object, he reached over with his own and handed it to the saleswoman.

"I was going to pay for that," Cat said. "It was a gift… from me."

"Same here. The chickens are a gift from me." He took the brown-paper-wrapped packages from her as they started the trek back to the car. "And it's rude to say no to a gift."

Their gazes clashed for a moment as he insisted on opening the door. Finally, she relented by smiling. "Okay, fine, this time. I do love the chickens."

As they rode back to Buckleberry Bend, the joking from earlier had ceased, but what replaced it was a companionable silence that he didn't mind at all. For the first time in a long time, his brain wasn't racing and his usual restlessness was strangely subdued.

Cat pulled into his driveway and put the car in park. He opened the door and prepared to turn his body to get his bad leg out and on the ground.

Before he could move, she reached over and kissed his cheek. "Thanks for a fun day," she said.

He rarely blushed, but damn if he didn't feel his cheeks go hot. He nodded quickly and got out of the car before she could notice.

"Preston," she said, calling him back. He bent over to see what she wanted. "Don't forget your sword."

"Thanks, chickie," he said with a wink, taking the package she handed him. That made her smile, and he couldn't help smiling back.

In the time it took for him to straighten up and wave, she was gone. He stood there, rubbing his cheek where she'd kissed it. And in that moment, he knew one thing. If it was possible to slay his dragons, he'd do it. For her.

Preston was headed back to the house when his cell rang. His father. He didn't want to answer. Didn't want to ruin the sense of almost complete happiness that he felt. Finally he decided to pick it up. Like a shot in the doctor's office, it was usually best to get anything having to do with his father over with as soon as possible.

"Hi Son," said the familiar voice.

"Hi, Vernon," Preston said. He simply couldn't muster *Dad* just then.

"Hey, my disability check still hasn't come in. Think you could spot me another hundred or so? Don't want them to shut off my water or anything."

Preston knew this had to stop. That his dad needed to return to rehab, and that every time Preston caved and gave him money, Preston was giving him an excuse not to go. But frankly, Pretson was tired. He didn't want to argue or strong arm him back to rehab or even *think* of his father right now. Or be reminded of his own problems which he'd somehow nearly managed to forget for a little while.

"I'll have my assistant pay your water bill," Preston said.

"And while you're at it," Vernon said, "could you have her put a little more into my account? Just till that check arrives."

Preston squeezed his eyes shut, hoping to shut out the bad feelings that were weaving their way in, disrupting his great mood.

"Sure, Vernon. I'll take care of it." When he hung up the phone, he was shaking a little. He had to sit for a minute on his front steps.

Vernon was a poison in his life. Preston had hoped that his father would change with the best resources but he doubted that would ever happen. His father served as a constant reminder of what could happen to someone who'd gone through hell and had become ensnared in the web of pain and addiction.

It had taken mere days—no, minutes—for Cat to slip under his skin. Slip into his heart and wash away his resolve. Hell, had she really ever left it? He knew in his gut this wonderful, horrible happiness wasn't real. He couldn't allow it for her sake.

Who was he kidding? Slaying those dragons was going to be impossible. He'd lost sight of his focus. He had to stop dreaming and fantasizing about fairy tales and work to protect her from himself.

Chapter Nine

"So we have a little problem," Cat said to her sister Maddie as she stepped into Maddie's office at their family's shoe company the next afternoon. She'd finished up work at the grade school and had offered to pick up Preston for his PT appointment.

Maddie looked up from the pile of multicolored square leather samples, ribbons, tape measures, and drawings in front of her on her worktable and smiled.

She'd been doing a lot of that lately. Smiling. Cat couldn't blame her, considering she was about to be married to the love of her life in just a few days, even if it was just a little annoying. Not that she would ever begrudge her sister her hard-won happiness. But still.

"Come in, sit down. Want some coffee? I just made a fresh pot." Maddie got up and cleared a bunch of drawings of shoes off a nearby chair. "What's the problem?"

Cat placed a long cardboard box on the worktable. "Open it."

Puzzled, Maddie opened the box. She pulled out

something long, lacy, and delicate attached to a crown of glittering rhinestones.

Maddie folded it back into the box and sat down. "I am not wearing Grandmeel's veil."

Cat threw her hands up in defense. "I'm the messenger. But just to let you know, she's regarding it as a gift. To refuse is to create problems."

"Cat. Please. Tell her I cannot wear that. Faux diamond tiara is not my style. And refusal or not, everything I do creates problems with Grandmeel."

"You'll have to tell her yourself. Because if you don't wear it, I'll have to. If I ever meet a guy I could marry."

"You're Grandmeel's favorite. So it's only natural she'd expect you to wear it. Which is also why you should tell her I am not wearing it because she won't hold a grudge against you if you refuse, but she definitely will toward me. And of course you're going to meet a great guy. Maybe even today, because there's someone here I want you to meet."

Cat wandered over to the window, which overlooked a tributary of the lake as it wound its way toward downtown. She was surprised to see Preston half leaning against a picnic table, cell phone to his ear. He was wearing form-fitting dress pants and a white dress shirt that fit elegantly over his muscular chest. A chest, she reminded herself, that she'd seen up close that fateful night a week ago. The memory of his hungry, all-consuming kisses made her bring her fingers to her lips as if those kisses were still imprinted there. The great time they'd had yesterday was such a contrast to anything they'd done before—it had been so much fun to just do something normal together, without the threat of war in the background or the tragedy of everything being different. In fact, they'd had so much fun they'd completely forgotten about buying a wedding gift.

"Cat?"

"Oh, sorry, Maddie. I was just—"

Suddenly her sister was behind her. "Staring at Preston." Maddie took hold of her sister's shoulders and shook. "This guy just might make you forget him."

Oh, right. She was losing track of her goal. "What guy?" she said, trying to sound interested.

Maddie pointed out the window. As they watched, another man strode up to Preston. Preston tucked his phone in his pocket and pushed up from the table. Cat saw the slightest wince as he straightened, one that was quickly masked by a smile. He heartily shook the guy's hand then drew him into a hug.

"Behold Brady Cosgrove, one of Nick's close friends from college. He's here for the wedding…but he came early to interview for the CEO job. He's coming for dinner tonight at Mom and Dad's. Grandmeel's really excited. She's got high hopes that you two will hit it off. And so do I."

Oh God. A group matchmaking effort. How pathetic was she, anyway?

Cat looked at the two men below. Both tall, strapping guys. Brady had lighter hair compared to Preston's deep brown, and it was wavy and longish compared to Preston's short, no-nonsense cut. He, like Preston, was definitely a man capable of turning heads. But Preston possessed the lethally proud bearing of a warrior, and it was even more evident in his work environment.

Sadly, there was only one man turning her head.

"So I spoke to Derrick," Maddie said, using the big-sister tone Cat knew so well. "According to him, you and Preston have been spending some time together lately. Do you think with your past history that's wise?"

"How much do you know?" Cat asked right off the bat. If her siblings had chatted, she could bet the ranch Maddie knew everything.

"Besides the fact that Derrick found you in Preston's lap? How could I not know about this?"

"You're getting married Saturday. My problems—"

"Still matter regardless of what's going on in my life. Don't you know that by now?"

Cat was grateful for her sister's concern, but she didn't want to burden her before the wedding. "We sort of made an arrangement."

"A what?" Maddie gave her the big-sister look she knew so well—the one loaded with disapproval…and perhaps pity.

"We agreed to let everyone think we were dating until the wedding so we didn't upset Derrick. I didn't want to do anything to ruin the wedding. In exchange, Preston offered to introduce me to a couple of nice guys he knew."

"Couldn't you have told Derrick the truth?"

Cat stared at her sister. "Remember the cowboy?"

Maddie cringed. "Okay, Derrick would have killed Preston. I get it. But he's going to anyway once he learns this is all a farce."

"Thus the plan to find me someone else."

"That is seriously effed up." The pitying look was definitely front and center now. "Oh, Cat. You're playing with fire. But you already know that."

Cat sighed. "It's complicated." Maddie had no clue how much. "But Maddie, we've spent some time together and I really feel like…like we're starting to communicate again." She felt a blush rise into her face. That sounded lame, but how could she tell her sister she'd felt things with him, sensed things, that made her think that maybe it was possible…

"Have you had a heart-to-heart with him? Did you find out why he ghosted on you?"

"No, but…"

"You always give people the benefit of the doubt. You always think the best of them, Cat, and it gets you hurt every time. All the more reason to step away from Preston and meet somebody else—someone *not* of Preston's choosing, because knowing him, I can't imagine the kind of man he'd choose for you. Probably someone seventy and completely unattractive."

You have no idea, Cat thought, remembering iPad man.

"I'm telling you," Maddie said, "Brady is a great guy from a great family. Nick says he has a heart of gold, and he's at the point in his life where he wants to settle down. Unlike Preston, who has a terrible track record with women."

Cat sat down on a comfortable sofa against the window. "I can't help thinking there's something he's not telling me. Something preventing him from getting close to me."

Her sister sighed the kind of sigh Cat knew meant advice was forthcoming. Lots of advice. "He's told you no in no uncertain terms. Maybe he needs time to get his shit together after all he's been through. And sometimes after a life-and-death experience, people just decide something's not right, you know?" She placed a hand on her shoulder. "Forget about him, Cat. Meet Brady. Turn your life in a new direction. Okay?"

Now it was Cat's turn to sigh. Maddie was practically begging. She knew her sister meant well and just wanted her to move on and be happy—like Maddie was. "Okay, fine. Introduce me." Maybe Maddie was right. It certainly wouldn't hurt to meet someone, would it? Besides, seeing Preston's reaction to her meeting a hot guy under the age of seventy would be very interesting.

Cat eventually left Maddie and wandered into her father's office, hoping to find Preston there. He was always punctual, but if they didn't hurry, he was going to miss PT. "Where's Dad?' Maddie asked after greeting Rebecca, the gray-haired receptionist who'd been working for her father since 1985.

"In a meeting with Pres—I mean Mr. Guthrie. They should be out in a minute. I swear, knowing you all since you've been children makes it all the more hard to believe you're all grown up now. Who knew that gorgeous stud muffin of a man used to be a wild boy who used to pull your braids and wipe boogers on your sleeve?"

Come to think of it, Preston did have the ability to torment her even way back then. "Do you mind if I grab some coffee while I wait?"

"Help yourself, dear."

Cat walked over to a coffeepot on a little table against the wall, but judging from the burned smell, it was at least a couple hours old. She made a mental reminder to have Santa bring her father a professional-grade coffee and tea brewer for Christmas. Or sooner. The idea of being able to buy something brought back memories of her botched job interview and a wave of panic that she had nothing else lined up. To distract herself, she poured a cup of the thick, black liquid.

"It's so nice to see you again," Rebecca said. "I hope you're doing okay after—um, *you know*. Besides being a little on the thin side, you're looking quite well."

Cat added powdered creamer, but dark grounds were swirling ominously around the cup.

So her broken engagement was now the event-that-will-not-be-spoken. "Thanks, but that was almost a year ago. I'm doing fine now." She liked Rebecca, but she had to find an excuse to leave before the prying started.

Rebecca leaned forward on her elbows and tapped her pen on a stack of papers. "My sister's got kids in Philadelphia, and she heard Robert's news."

Cat stopped stirring and looked up. "What news?"

"Oh, I thought surely you knew. He's getting married

over Labor Day weekend. And his fiancée…she's pregnant."

"Oh, *that* news." Her hand was shaking so bad, she set down the cup for fear she'd drop it. Pretending to be busy with the coffee, she tried adding sugar, which poured out in a large dump, making it essentially undrinkable, but at this point, she just wanted to survive long enough to bolt out of here. She forced a pleasant smile. "Of course I wish them the best of luck." She casually took a sip of the slurry and couldn't help choking. "I'll wait for Preston in the break room."

She forced herself to walk at a normal pace into the break room and closed the door. At three thirty in the afternoon, it was empty, so she collapsed into the nearest chair and rubbed her temples. She didn't still love Robert. If anything, she felt a sense of relief at having dodged something that would have made her miserable in the long run. Mostly she was angry with herself for picking someone so totally wrong. And yes, she was jealous…but not of him. Of his happiness. Of the fact that he had a new baby on the way, the start of a new life she was nowhere near achieving.

"Dammit," she said out loud, "I should have taken that trip to Hawaii when I had the chance. Why didn't I?"

Anger turned to sadness. She wanted babies to love, a home of her own, and a life with someone you loved more than anyone. Who loved you for who you were, not for who he wanted you to be.

Instead, here she was, living back in Buckleberry Bend with her parents, out of a job and alone. Ready to watch her sister walk down the aisle with a man whom she was crazy about and who was clearly crazy about her.

To cure her urge toward self-pity, she took another slug of the disgusting coffee.

Someone cleared their throat. Cat looked up, coffee suddenly sloshing onto her blouse.

The woman standing by the coffee maker was blond

and buxom, with perfect makeup, her hair done up in a professional-looking bun. "I—I remember you from...from the hospital," Cat said. "Lacey, right?"

Preston's personal assistant. She'd been the one to call Cat and tell her Preston was injured, that he'd hurt his knee and suffered a concussion and had lost enough blood to require a transfusion.

Cat had dropped everything that day and left. She'd still been working in Philly, and had gotten in her car and driven the two and a half hours to Walter Reed. She'd sat by his side day and night for two days until he'd finally woken up. Lacey had been there, too, and she'd seemed to be a faithful friend, a longtime employee who hadn't intimidated Cat even though she was stunningly beautiful.

At the time Cat had interpreted Preston's stoic demeanor, his distance, as coming from someone who'd been through a huge shock. Who was critically ill. Looking back, however, she'd missed all the signs that he was about to kiss her off. How much Lacey knew of Preston's personal life she had no idea.

In the break room, Lacey walked over to Cat. She was wearing a beautifully tailored gray business suit and classy high heels Cat herself would have been struggling to walk in. "Great to see you again, Cat." She smiled and extended her hand.

"You, too," Cat said. "I'm here to drive Preston to PT. But he said his assistant was coming, so since you're here, maybe you don't need me to—"

The door swung open. Preston stood there for a moment, taking in Cat and Lacey, looking a little thrown off guard. "I see you two have met." He paused. Sort of uncomfortably. Cleared his throat. "Hi, sweetheart."

Cat felt her face heat up. She was actually a little shocked, but mostly pleased. He'd called her sweetheart, in public! Her heart felt a little swollen; her breath came a little fast. It was a small acknowledgment, a baby step. It proved they were finding their way back to each other. Their day in Charlotte had been amazing, and it really had broken down some barriers between them.

"I've missed you," Preston said. Cat looked up to see his gaze directed not at her but at Lacey. What? He'd just called Lacey *sweetheart*?

"Well, I've missed you too, boss," Lacey said, her tone all business. "Guess we better get going to that appointment of yours—"

Preston moved forward, and right before Cat's eyes, he grabbed Lacey around the waist, dipped her a little, and planted a kiss on her lips. Not just any kiss, either. This kiss was big and bold, a grand gesture. Romantic and dramatic at the same time.

Cat blinked. Her mouth fell open. *Sweetheart?* A ballroom dip? That kind of kiss was *not* an I-really-missed-my-personal-assistant kind of kiss at all—unless he was getting *really* personal with her.

Cat must be hallucinating from those coffee grounds she just swallowed, because Preston couldn't possibly have just kissed this woman. Not after the fantastic time they'd had together yesterday. The lunch, the ice cream, the shopping. She'd thought they were making inroads. Starting to communicate. She'd been a fool.

What was going on here? Preston couldn't possibly be... oh God. He was fucking his PA. Of course he was. It had never even occurred to her, naive, trusting person that she was. Unbelievable.

She turned toward the door. It was time to go. This amusement park ride was making her seasick with all the ups and downs, and she couldn't keep spinning in circles. She needed off the carousel.

Lacey stepped forward, blocking her exit. She folded her arms, looking no-nonsense, professional and polished. "Preston," she said, casting a sympathetic glance at Cat.

He'd embarrassed Lacey, which led Cat to think she was a decent person, but who knew?

"Yes, babe?" he said.

"I have no idea what's going on, but it needs to stop now. I won't take part in whatever you're trying to do here."

Cat looked from Lacey to Preston. The color in his face was high. She knew him well enough to know he was displeased. He was casting frowning glances at his PA, but she was just standing there rolling her eyes.

"Tell her the truth," Lacey said, tapping her foot.

Preston rubbed his neck. Shuffled his feet. Looked at the floor. "You know the truth, Lacey. It's okay to admit we've been seeing each other."

Cat forced herself to maintain an even gait as she headed for the door. She had no idea what this was about but she'd had enough. She'd thrown open the door and stepped into the corridor when she overheard Lacey saying, "If you don't tell her, I will."

As soon as Cat reached the end of hall, Lacey caught up with her and motioned her into the supply room. Her clear blue eyes looked troubled, probably from guilt. She reached out a hand and gripped Cat's arm tightly. "He's never kissed me before *ever*. He's my boss. I don't know what just got into him."

"You don't owe me any explanations." Cat was done here, and she wanted to leave. Now.

Lacey tried to put a hand on her shoulder, but Cat stepped away and opened the door. "Look, Cat," she said, "there's nothing between us, I swear."

"I'm sorry, Lacey," Cat said. "I don't know what to believe anymore."

"If you don't believe me, check his wallet."

The cryptic answer pissed her off. "What?"

"Check his wallet," Lacey said. "I had to open it when he was in the hospital. What you find there might surprise you."

Cat left, only to run right into Preston, who was standing in the hall with the man from outside near the picnic table that Maddie wanted her to meet. Dammit, right when she was one door away from the stairs. She struggled to take deep, calming breaths and paste a smile on her face when inside she felt like she was coming down with the plague. Or anything else that made you feel like living death.

In contrast to Preston's concrete-hard stare, this man's gaze raked over her in blatant appreciation. He was even more handsome up close, with sandy brown hair and a muscular build, but lacking the foreboding power Preston carried like a second skin.

"I'm Brady Cosgrove." Preston's companion flashed a brilliant white smile and offered his hand, which she took as she returned a forced smile. "I'm interviewing for the new CEO position." Maybe he wasn't as tall or as large as Preston, but he certainly was more pleasant-looking, as Preston wore a deep scowl that would've scared her five-year-olds half to death.

"Catherine Kingston. Maddie's sister." She could handle saying her name but beyond that, God only knew. She needed to get out of here as soon as possible before she lost it. To scold herself, she gave herself a harsh reminder that she asked for this. For all of it, by getting tangled up with Preston again. But when the chips were down, Kingstons didn't disappoint other Kingstons, so she faked a smile so this man wouldn't think any of her family were crazed.

"I know who you are," Brady said. "You work for the *Inquirer*. I read the piece your paper did on the revitalization of Kingston Shoes. It's what first brought the company to my notice. I picked up the phone and called Nick and…here I am."

"That was a great piece," she said, still fake-smiling. "I'm so glad you found it useful."

He had golden brown eyes that reminded her of a tiger. His hand lingered until she broke contact.

Now it was Preston's turn to clear his throat. "We need to be going, Brady. I'll look over your file and present your candidacy to the board." He looked over at Lacey, who was standing behind Cat. "You'll escort Mr. Cosgrove out, won't you, Lacey?"

Preston steered Cat down the hall, away from the stairs and her precious escape, before she could even say good-bye. He walked so fast, she had to run a little to keep up despite his impaired gait. At the opposite end of the hall, he got into the elevator and held his hand across the door opening so she could get in. She stared at him from the hallway and crossed her arms.

"Do you actually think I'm getting in that elevator with you?"

His thick brows shot up.

Cat stared at him in awe. Did he think she was dense? Clueless? Or too reluctant to rock the boat?

Oh, she was going to rock it, all right. And he was going to need a life jacket to keep himself afloat.

Chapter Ten

"Cat, please get in the elevator." Preston held out his other hand to her. It was like encouraging a feral cat toward some food. One about to bite his hand off with her fangs.

"No way."

"Cat, please," he whispered. That gossipy administrative assistant was right around the corner. If she caught wind of their heated words, it would be all over the building by quitting time. He shot a glance down the hall, where two associates chatted as they walked toward the elevator.

"Please get in so we can talk about this."

"I'm not talking to you in a place where there's no escape."

At that moment, Rebecca walked toward them to use the water cooler, which was across from the elevator. She was thirsty, all right. For gossip.

Reluctantly, Cat got in. As soon as the doors snapped shut he punched the stop button. "Okay, let's talk."

She stood against the far wall, as far away from him as possible, seeming to choose her words carefully. "How could my brother have picked such a dishonorable man for his best friend?"

That one word froze his blood. Because no matter what bad traits he had, being dishonorable wasn't one of them. He'd led his life with honor, served with honor. Pushed her away for her own sake. Made a stupid attempt to do so now with Lacey because after yesterday, Cat was getting too close to wearing down his defenses. And if he allowed that, it would be a disaster for both of them.

"Lacey's not my girlfriend." He rubbed the back of his neck. "She never was."

"You're insane." Her lip was quivering. "W-why did you just do that—kiss her? I'm done playing games, Preston. I want the truth. All of it."

Oh God. He'd made a royal mess of things. He'd seen Lacey and had the sudden, stupid idea that he could use her to push Cat away. Prevent her from working her way even further into his system.

Guilt ripped through him. How could he tell her the truth? That the leg injury was nothing, nothing compared to what had happened to him on the inside. And he wasn't going to let her anywhere near that.

He was ashamed at what he'd done. He kept hurting her because of his inability to stay away from her. He kept falling under her spell. In his house the other night, when he kissed her. In Charlotte, when they'd talked and laughed and had such a great day together. He had to let her know that anything between them could never be. Then get the hell away from her before he betrayed himself again.

Cat's eyes were watery. "After you were hurt, I thought you were going to die," she said. "You'd been in shock, transfused. I prayed, I begged God you'd make it back to the States." She paused. "I was too stupid to see the signs that you were about to dump me. I can handle that you don't want me. But why didn't you just tell me the truth?"

Misery swamped him. He didn't want to be like that bastard she'd almost married. Make her feel unwanted and unloved when she was the sweetest, sexiest woman he'd ever known. Yet he couldn't tell her the truth. He couldn't. But he had to say something.

"After my injury, I couldn't tell you that I wanted to go back to being friends. And I didn't want your pity. You know as well as I do you never would have abandoned me in the condition I was in. It would have made it impossible for me to tell you my—change of heart."

"You're saying you wanted to call it quits before you injured your knee, but then the injury made it impossible for you to tell me that?"

"Come on, Cat. We all know how loyal you are. I tried to be the kind of guy who could settle down with just one woman but I—couldn't. People can't change their basic makeup. I'm sorry."

Awkwardly, he did the only thing he could think of, he tried to put his arm on her shoulder, but she swiped it away. In the process, her purse tumbled off her arm, lipsticks and pens and loose change scattering everywhere. She ignored the mess, pushing a button on the control panel that made the elevator start to descend.

"We had a great day in Charlotte," Preston said. "I hope we'll always be friends. I—I did that dumb thing with Lacey to show you that we can never be more than that, Cat. I'm sorry."

"Whatever, Preston. When I knew you before, I trusted you, but now I don't know who you are. Because you're not really a friend if you ghost out on someone without explanation, and you sure as hell are not a friend if you lie."

She punched the open door button rapid-fire until the door finally released. Without a backward glance or stopping to pick up any of her things, she ran out of the elevator.

"Cat, wait." She didn't heed his calls. He thought about limping after her, but what comfort could he offer her after he'd just dropped that bombshell? Groups of people in the lobby stared at him. One woman watched Cat run for the door and cast him a judgmental glance as he stood in the elevator. He felt shell-shocked. His limbs wouldn't move. He had the feeling that he'd cut off the only thing in his life that truly mattered, and he'd done it willingly, fool that he was.

Somehow, he managed to push the second-floor button and mercifully, the door snapped shut. He managed to pick up most of Cat's stuff by pushing his bad leg over to the side and bending his good knee, but it was a real struggle to right himself. He walked out of the elevator dragging her purse and his pride, and made it past Rebecca's desk, which was mercifully empty, into the office where they'd been letting him work. He collapsed behind the desk, releasing a painful breath. His whole chest hurt. Hell, his entire body ached. He'd fucked this up for good. Which was what he wanted, right? He didn't want her in his life. He would only ruin her sweetness, her optimism. It couldn't be. He dragged his fingers through his hair and held his head in his hands.

"I'm glad you're finally showing what you feel for that woman."

He jerked his head up to find Lacey sitting on a couch across the room.

"What the hell are you still doing here?"

"Go ahead, fire me, but I'm not leaving until you hear from me just what an a-hole you are."

He winced at her words, because they were true. "Go to hell."

She stood and walked up to the desk. The woman may have had soft curves in all the right places but on the inside, she was all spikes and nails. "You're a fool, Preston. Cat still loves you. I can see that you care about her, too."

"Who died and made you a psychiatrist?"

"You don't need to be a psychiatrist to know that, only a human being. But for you, maybe that's a bit of a stretch."

He didn't know how to do love, because he'd never had it. But that didn't mean he didn't still crave it like a junkie, with every fiber of his being. It was better for him not to have it. He would only destroy it, and he'd never forgive himself if he took her down with him.

"Preston! You're being an idiot."

He blew out a big breath. "You're right about that, Lace. You are right about that. On top of everything else, Cat and I are supposed to be pretend-dating this week and I really screwed that up, too."

He looked up at her, his best employee. He'd hired her years ago when she'd tried to pick him up in a bar when she was only seventeen and had been desperate to get off the streets. Last December, she'd gotten her BS in finance, and he was preparing to promote her to a company position more tailored to her new skill set. If he didn't kill her first.

"I have time to listen," she said gently. "If you don't fire me, that is."

"I'd love to fire you, but you know too damn much about me."

A knock sounded on the open door. Preston looked up to see Brady Cosgrove standing there with a half grin on his face.

How much had he heard?

"Hey, I wanted to tell you the Kingston family has invited me to dinner tonight, and Mr. K. told me to tell you that you're invited, too."

Great. Just what he wanted to do.

"He told me you're dating Cat, but...did I just hear right? You're not really dating her?"

Fuck. And he'd thought his day couldn't circle the bowl

any lower. "We've been friends for a long time. She—needed a date for the wedding, after she suffered a broken engagement last summer. So I'm just filling in for her. To—save her the embarrassment." God, he needed a drink. How did he just make that shit up? Oh, he didn't. Because that much was mostly true.

"Great. Because I think she's amazing. You wouldn't mind then if I got to know her a little better?"

Lacey shot Preston a you've-got-to-be-kidding look.

"That would be up to Catherine," he said. "You'll have to excuse me, Brady. I've got urgent business." He turned to Lacey. "I need you to drive me somewhere."

Lacey crossed her arms and raised one perfectly arched brow. "Does this mean I'm not fired?"

• • •

Cat ran out to her car, sucking in big gulps of fresh air. She dropped her forehead onto the glass of the driver's window, hoping its coolness would seep into her brain and calm her down. But it was already burning hot from the cheery spring sunshine that surrounded her like a suffocating blanket. She realized too late what a stupid idea it had been to leave the contents of her upset purse, since she'd just basically thrown away her car keys.

She heard a strong male voice behind her.

"Forget your keys?"

Cat swiped at her wet cheeks. She whirled around, expecting Preston but finding Brady instead. He wore a kind look on his face.

Something made her tell him the truth. "To be honest, I was upset and my purse spilled, and I ran out without bothering to pick anything up."

He grinned. He had nice eyes, kind of warm and twinkly.

"Look, you don't have to explain anything to me. Can I give you a ride somewhere?"

She wanted nothing more than to escape before someone like her dad came barreling out and saw her in this state. "I'd appreciate that a lot."

He walked her over to a black Mercedes SUV and helped her in.

Cat tried to focus on the rich leather smell of the interior, its spotlessness, and the abundant cool air blowing in as he cranked up the AC. But Preston's words kept running through her head. *I wanted to go back to being friends. And I didn't want your pity.*

It proved what he'd tried to tell her all along, that he didn't have a clue about being in a real relationship or about accepting help when he was vulnerable.

She realized Brady was talking to her. "Oh, sorry. Turn here." Morning Glory Lane wasn't far from downtown Buckleberry Bend with its rows of art galleries and antique shops, the pancake house and the coffee shop, and the grassy park with its statue of the first mayor, General Krandall Pervis Pritchett. Today nothing seemed quaint. Everything felt stifling. She longed to be alone on the grassy island a short kayak ride from her parents' backyard, where it always seemed she could row out to and be alone and escape life for a while.

Sadly, she was no longer a lonesome teenager with braces and thick glasses, paddling out with a book to spend the day with to forget her troubles.

Love required believing you are worthy of being loved. No matter how much she cared for Preston, if he wasn't able to love himself, forgive himself, share what he was going through with her, his pride would always stand in their way.

Brady glanced at her from the driver's seat. "I'm really looking forward to dinner at your house tonight."

She smiled at him before opening the door to get out. He'd been kind to her, and it wasn't his fault things were so messed up. "Thanks for the ride. I'll see you later."

He held her back with his words. "Look, Cat, I know you're not really dating Preston."

She turned slowly to face him. "How do you know that?"

"I overheard Preston talking to his PA. I want to say that whatever it is you're going through, if you need to bend someone's ear, you can always bend mine."

Cat thought about that, and realized she probably did have a shortage of people who were patient enough to listen. There was no way she would dump her problems on Maddie now just before the wedding. Her practical older sister, Liz, was recovering from her own divorce and would have no tolerance for such nonsense. And Finn was sick of her mooning over Preston a long time more than what was sensible.

"Thanks, Brady. And thanks for the ride." It had been a long time since someone was simply—kind to her. Brady had seen she was distressed and didn't ask questions, yet he seemed caring.

So unlike Preston. Too bad Brady was not the one she wanted.

Chapter Eleven

Cat showered and dressed in a sleeveless blouse, ankle pants, and cute sandals. She put on a pair of silver dangly earrings and straightened her hair. She had no idea how she was going to tolerate pretending to show Preston affection in front of her family, but she was not going to let him—or anyone— know how upset she was. She could cry into her pillow later, but for now, she was going to act like the happiest woman in the world if that's what it took to keep the peace in the final days before Maddie's wedding.

All she had to do was survive this dinner and tomorrow's planned afternoon at the lake before Saturday's wedding. Then they would all disband, and she'd only have to see him at occasional family events, probably involving Maddie and Nick's or Derrick and his wife Jenna's kids. Even thinking of seeing him in the future, with other women, or one day with someone he loved, a wife and children, sent sword slashes into her heart.

Cat met her mother in the kitchen as she was preparing marinade for chicken shish kebabs. Liz sat at the island, chopping vegetables. She looked really pretty, wearing a black sleeveless dress with gold hoops that looked elegant against her straight shoulder-length black hair. Grandmeel sat, too, slicing fruit for fruit salad.

"Where's Samuel tonight?" Cat asked her. Grandmeel was dating her long-lost love, Nick's grandpa, who worked doing shoe design at the company with Maddie, and it had done wonders in taking a bit of the edge off her personality. She wished for that reason he could be here with them tonight. Left to her own devices, God only knew what Grandmeel would say.

"He had to meet with a client, so he stayed behind so Maddie could come," Amelia said. "He may show up later."

"Oh, hello, Cat." Her mom whizzed by and gave her a kiss on the cheek as she pulled a bowl of marinated chicken out of the fridge. "Could you help me skewer these kebabs? I want to have them all ready to go on the grill."

Cat washed her hands. As she sat down next to Liz at a stool around the large island, she gave her a little nudge in the ribs. "With all the wedding commotion, I've barely talked to you lately." Not for the first time, she wondered how her sister was handling Maddie's newfound happiness. She was sure Liz was happy for Maddie, like they all were, but going through all the wedding preparations had to remind her of her own wedding three years ago and her crushing divorce after just a year.

"The news of the day," Grandmeel said, "is that Maddie doesn't care to wear my beautiful veil. Catherine, perhaps you'll wear it one day."

Uh-oh. She focused on skewering tomatoes and peppers and chicken onto the kebab sticks. "Um, maybe, Grandmeel. But don't count on that anytime soon. I mean, after last year and all…" She felt a sudden solidarity with her oldest sister. With her failed engagement and Liz's failed marriage, they had reason to team together to avoid The Veil.

"Don't remind us, dear," Grandmeel said. "Lord, it kills me to think of all that fine crystal and china we had to return." Grandmeel paused in her slicing long enough to emit a heavy sigh. "Perhaps it was for the better. I never liked the mathematician."

"An actuary," Liz said. "He calculated insurance risks."

"Lord have mercy, that makes me yawn just thinking about what the hell kind of job that possibly could be."

"Don't worry, Grandmeel," Liz said, tossing an evil big-sister wink at Cat. "Preston Guthrie's back in town helping Dad find a new CEO. He and Cat have rekindled their romance. He's a nice guy with a great job, right?"

Cat shot her sister a look, but Liz just quirked a corner of her mouth. Now was not the time to put her in a spot with Grandmeel, as Liz was so fond of doing.

Grandmeel set down her knife and addressed Cat. "About Preston Guthrie. I want to see you happy with a good man who treats you like a queen and who hails from good stock. Is that so much to ask? How can a man from his sordid background possibly know how to treat a woman or be a good husband? Honestly, Catherine, you must see how something like that could never work."

Oh, this was too much. Her emotions were too ragged and raw. She was going to start bawling again for sure. She grabbed the onions from Liz and started chopping just in case.

Cat's mom spoke. "Your dad and I were excited to hear that you and Preston have mended your fences. Weddings do that. They bring people together." It was getting really hard to focus when lies were building upon lies, and guilt was creeping in. "Besides, I like Preston," her mother continued. "He's a high-quality man, always has been. He's a West Point grad, a successful businessman, and a war hero, Amelia. Not to mention a nice guy. I don't hold his background against him at all."

"You can't change people," Grandmeel said. "They can't overcome their backgrounds. If you're raised in an atmosphere of abuse, you abuse, if for no other reason than you don't know any differently."

"That's not true," Cat said in a soft voice. "Some people would do anything to overcome their backgrounds." She wondered if that included pushing away people they cared about.

Cat bit her lip to avoid saying any more. She had to give her family some warning that it was over between them. "There's no need to worry. We're — taking it slow. He's not the type to settle down."

"That's what everyone said about your father, too," Cat's mom said.

The knife slipped, and Cat almost cut herself. Liz took it away from her and pushed the bowl of chicken closer so she could go back to skewering the kebabs. "Dad was a — a *womanizer*?"

Her father, a tall man with gray hair who wore an apron his employees got him that said, "My barbecue will knock your shoes off," walked into the kitchen. He looked a hundred times better than he did last summer, when he was recovering from a stroke. Even had a tan from the few rounds of golf he played each Wednesday. He kissed her mom on the cheek. "There's only one woman for me."

"Don't avoid the question, Dad," Liz said. "You dated around a lot before you met Mom?"

He shrugged. "I was confused. Your mother set me straight."

"He means I threatened him," she said.

"When necessary, that's what true love does." Her dad winked at his daughters and went back out the door with the chicken to man his grill.

"So, about that veil," Liz said, at last finally steering the conversation away from the topic of Preston. "I'd love to wear it someday, if you'll let me, Grandmeel." She winked at Cat and whispered, "Problem solved. Because the day I marry again will be the day Buckleberry Bend gets a McDonald's."

Cat smiled. That would likely be a while. Every year since the fifties, the city council had staunchly voted against having any fast-food establishments in town.

"Finally," Grandmeel said. "One of my granddaughters is showing some sense."

Cat's mom, who never missed much of anything, came to stand behind her daughters. "Life has a way of surprising us, my dears. You never know what can happen. Maybe in a year, both of you will be fighting over wearing that veil."

Cat waited for Grandmeel to say something about Liz being divorced or not having any current prospects for a husband, but she didn't. She also didn't take the opportunity to complain more about Cat's failed engagement. She'd even said Robert was boring. Cat knew the subtle changes were the result of Samuel's influence. Lately, Grandmeel was happier than she'd ever seen her. Not that she'd had a complete personality transplant, but there were definite improvements.

So maybe Grandmeel had just disproved her own theory. Maybe people could change after all.

Cat happened to be coming down the stairs after fetching Grandmeel's eyeglasses when Nick and Maddie walked through the front door with Preston.

"Hi, sis," Maddie said, giving Cat a hug. "How's your headache?"

"My headache?" She didn't have one now, not that she didn't rule out getting one any moment during a long evening pretending to like Preston in front of her entire family.

"Yeah, Preston said Brady gave you a ride home because your head was throbbing so bad you couldn't drive."

"Oh, that headache. Gone." She waved her hand in the air. "Thanks to the miracle of Advil."

"We brought your car back. Here are your keys."

"Thanks for doing that," she said as she set them down on the hall table.

Preston walked forward to greet her. "Hi, honey," he said, kissing her lightly on the cheek. "And here's your purse that you, um, forgot."

She took the purse and said, "Hi to you, too," with a big, fake smile that really was giving her a headache.

Nick greeted her warmly with a hug. "Hey, sis." He slapped Preston playfully on the back. "Who'd have thought you'd be the one to break through to this guy?"

"She's the only woman for me." Preston forced another smile and wrapped an arm around Cat, who tried not to feel as stiff as a paper doll.

Fortunately, Preston and Nick began talking business and were soon deep in conversation. "Let me get you that business card," Preston said, pulling out his wallet.

His wallet. Cat's heart suddenly knocked hard against her rib cage as she remembered Lacey's words. *If you don't believe me, check his wallet.* What could a wallet possibly tell her about Preston that she didn't already know? There went her flair for the dramatic, acting up again. The bottom line was he still wanted to call it quits. She just had to focus on surviving this dinner and the wedding festivities this weekend until this nightmare was over.

They all gathered around the fire pit in the backyard, Brady and Derrick and Jenna joining the rest of them. Dad poured everyone prosecco in honor of Maddie and Nick's big upcoming weekend. Cat was grateful for something else to focus on to dull the sting of her hurt and her general state of pissed-offedness at Preston, who sat next to her but seemed to act as awkwardly as she—not touching her and speaking to her as little as possible.

"I love weddings," her mother said on a sigh. Rosalyn Kingston was a crier, worse than Cat, so Cat braced herself for the speech she could see coming. Her mom raised her glass of prosecco while Henry beamed at her side. "We're so proud of you, Maddie and Nick, and are so looking forward to your wedding weekend. Also, your wedding has helped Cat and Preston come together. Preston, it's so wonderful to see you again. I'm glad you and Cat worked out your differences. And Henry's been so grateful for your help in the CEO search."

Preston raised his glass. "It's been a pleasure to help out, ma'am. We've had some great candidates."

Rosalyn raised her glass in the direction of her oldest daughter. "Liz, we're so happy to have you back with us from Africa, and so glad you've decided to stay in town to practice. Love you too, honey." She turned to Derrick and Jenna. "Last but not least, we are so looking forward to the new addition to our family in just a few short months."

Derrick took up his wife's hand and kissed it, and she beamed at him. Everyone raised their glasses and drank to the toast, Cat draining her prosecco like there was a fire nearby. She loved her family, was happy for everyone, but she wanted to be here tonight about as much as she loved black-eyed peas.

"Catherine's got a degree in journalism," Grandmeel told Brady in front of everyone. "Worked for the *Philadelphia Inquirer* until recently. She just interviewed for a position at the *Charlotte Herald*. My father and grandfather were both newspapermen. The talent runs in the family. As I always say, Kingstons were born to educate the world."

"About that," Cat said, cutting off her grandmother at the

pass. "I-I'm thinking of switching my occupation. Becoming a teacher." Wow, she'd finally come out and said it. She'd never put it into words before, but…yeah. There it was. The truth.

"Lord, child, that prosecco's gone straight to your head," Grandmeel said. "Teaching is the lowest-paid profession anywhere."

"I've been substituting this week for the kindergarten class at Buckleberry Elementary. It's a real challenge."

"Honestly, Catherine," Grandmeel said, "changing your mind about marriage, changing your career…you're coming across as very indecisive. All this mind-changing is getting expensive."

Cat turned red, embarrassed to be scolded in front of the family. Just when she opened her mouth to muster a reply, Preston spoke. "People are entitled to change their minds, Amelia. Sometimes it's a matter of finding out what you don't like. Whatever Cat decides, I know she'll throw her entire heart into it like she always does."

"That's easy for you to say," Grandmeel said. "You're not paying for more education."

"I wouldn't expect anyone to pay for my education," Cat said. "I'd do it myself."

"We'll support Cat in whatever she decides," her dad said.

"Well, she'd better hurry up," Grandmeel said. "She's not getting any younger." Liz shifted uncomfortably in her seat, undoubtedly taking Grandmeel's comment as an insult to herself as well. Cat looked at her mother, who rolled her eyes and subtly poured the half glass that was left of her dad's prosecco into her own glass.

Preston must have been in the mood to spar, because he said, "The Kingston women are like fine wine, Amelia. They only improve with age."

Liz quietly lifted her glass to him from her seat off to the side. But Cat just cleared her throat. "I'm going to get the

watermelon," she said. "Be right back, sugar," she said, patting
Preston on the knee.

"Take your time, sweetness," he called back.

On impulse, she turned and lifted the nearly full glass of
prosecco her mom had just set down on the table and took it
for herself.

· · ·

"Preston, another beer?" Brady asked, reaching into the
cooler for another bottle.

"No, thanks," Preston said. "I'm still working on this one."

"You're a one-beer kind of guy, huh? Must be a
lightweight."

What, was this guy back in college, competing for how
many beers he could slug down in one night? He clearly never
had to handle a belligerent, out-of-his-mind drunk father who
was about to beat the shit out of his mother and force him to
go to bed. And if the guy told one more lacrosse story from
his time at Duke, Preston was going to hurl.

No, one beer was fine with him, thanks. He'd keep his wits
about him.

"So, Brady," Henry said as he dipped a chip into the
homemade guacamole and sat down on a cushioned deck
chair. "Tell us a little about where you'd see Kingston Shoes
headed under your leadership."

"Well, sir, I'd do everything I can to up the productivity. To
guarantee the workers a decent salary and to get your shoes
known across the nation. Maddie and Nick's grandfather
are a great design team. Now you need great marketing to
get the product out there. My father always used to say to
us kids growing up, work hard and work smart, meaning that
efficiency is the key to building up the company."

Brady had all the perfect answers. He came from the

perfect family. He possessed everything Cat could want, had everything her family was looking for, and was clearly crazy about her. Preston wanted to take him out of the job applicant pool just for that.

Cat opened the sliding door to the house, carrying a full tray of watermelon. As she headed down the few stairs to the deck, her sandal caught, and she lost her balance. The watermelon tipped and pieces began to slide off the tray.

Preston struggled to stand up with such force, his chair tipped over backward with a resounding *thud*. Before he could lumber over to help, Brady was beside her, grasping her by the elbow and catching her, another hand steadying the tray. Preston's damn leg had tripped him up and slowed him down as usual.

"Hey there, beautiful," Brady whispered loud enough Preston could hear. Then out loud, "Wouldn't want you to fall."

Grandmeel picked up Preston's chair. In a low voice, she said, "Now, wouldn't want you rushing over there and tripping on the watermelon seeds. You might hurt your good leg."

"With all respect, Amelia," Preston said, "I'm used to dodging land mines, so I don't think a couple of slippery seeds are going to trip me up." Preston barely registered her reply. Because Brady had helped Cat steady herself and was still touching her arm. He swore he saw him whisper something in her ear and sure enough, saw color rise to her face.

Shit. The man was making a play for her right in front of him.

Cat righted herself. "Thanks, Brady," she said. "Glad I'm okay, but I'm afraid half the watermelon isn't."

Brady bent down and started picking up the fallen melon and throwing it into the trash, something else Preston couldn't help with.

"I'll go back into the house and get some more," Cat said.

Preston was about to say he'd help her when Brady said it instead. And accompanied her into the kitchen.

"I'm so glad Brady's interviewing for our CEO job," Grandmeel said. "We need a smart, tough, and aggressive leader."

"He certainly is skilled," Preston said. *But he'd better not be using those skills on Cat.*

Cat's father tossed Preston a deferring look. "I appreciate the hard work you've put into narrowing down the CEO candidates, son. I know how hard you've been working at it."

Preston forced himself to focus on Mr. Kingston's words instead of wondering what the hell Brady was up to with Cat in the kitchen. He managed to crack a smile that felt as if he were moving his muscles through layers of caked-on mud. "Yes, sir. We'll for sure find a person who's a great fit for the company. Dedicated, hardworking, and shares your mission. I want to help you find someone who appreciates the way you all make your shoes. Who understands that quality does appeal over quantity."

He wasn't 100 percent sure Brady understood that. Oh, he was all about productivity, but the methods he'd use to get the company up to speed seemed to indicate he'd take away local jobs for automation and outsourcing.

"Are you saying some people interviewing for the position want us to use machines to speed up the shoemaking?" Derrick asked.

"Productivity is important," Nick said. "But Kingston Shoes were and always will be handmade." He turned to Henry. "I told you Preston had a good grip on the company's mission."

Yes, he did. But right now, the only mission Preston saw Brady having was to get Cat laid. A mission Preston didn't like one bit. "If you'll excuse me, I'm going to make a trip to the restroom."

When he entered the kitchen, Cat and Brady were standing at the island. Brady was cutting pieces of watermelon, and Cat was arranging them on the tray. And they were laughing.

"Hey, Preston," Cat said. "Need anything?"

"Just to talk to you," Preston said, taking her by the arm and leading her out of the kitchen. "Would you excuse us a minute?"

That's when Preston realized he was sweating. He couldn't wait another minute to tell her the truth. That he'd made that dumb move with Lacey today out of panic and stupidity. That he'd never wanted to let Cat go. That all he'd ever wanted was to have her, and how could he have her when he was in such a shit state of mind? When everything about his world was different now and he didn't even know who the hell he was anymore. Yet he had to tell her. Because he could not let this aggressive shithead walk in and take over.

"What is it?" Cat asked. Her tone was irritated. Her eyes held an impassive, hardened look he'd never seen before.

"Cat, I—"

"Oh, before you start, I want you to know there's no need for you to try to fix me up with anyone else. Brady's asked me out. I like him a lot."

He tried not to show his shock, his surprise. His *devastation*. Everything had turned out exactly as he'd planned. He'd rejected her, hurt her so she'd give him up for good, and found her a better man. Someone who was hale and hearty, from a better family, and who fit in perfectly with hers.

"That's...great, Cat. It's just what you wanted."

He searched her eyes for any signs she was calling his bluff, but she was smiling sweetly, her look expectant. Like she was excited she'd finally met an upstanding guy who was a gentleman and who treated her like she deserved to be treated.

Everything he wasn't or couldn't ever be. The guacamole

and chips he just ate tossed sickly in his stomach.

"What were you going to tell me?" she asked.

He broke his hold on her and turned back to head back to the kitchen "N-nothing. Just wondering if taking me to PT before heading to school was going to work for you tomorrow." Later tomorrow afternoon the wedding party was meeting at the lodge at the lake for fun and festivities before the big day on Saturday.

"I'm already packed for the weekend and I'll pick you up at eight sharp. Sound okay?"

"Great. Everything sounds great. Thanks."

Too bad nothing, absolutely nothing, felt great inside.

· · ·

Liz opened the screen door and walked in with an empty pitcher of iced tea. Cat was sitting at the island after sending Brady out with the watermelon, trying to figure out what the hell had just happened. Over the past week, she'd tried to wear Preston down with compassion, with confrontation, and now she'd resorted to primitive caveman tactics—good old-fashioned jealousy. She felt sick. He'd backed down, seemed happy for her. Shit, why did she go and do that?

"Wow, you never told me you had a love triangle thing going on," Liz said.

"What are you talking about?"

"Maddie already told me you're not really dating Preston. But is it warm in here?" She fanned her face with her hands. "Because he's throwing you enough heated glances to send the fire pit up in flames."

"We had a fight. The heated glances are probably from wishing he were anywhere but here."

"What is there to fight about if you're not really dating?"

"It's super complicated."

Liz sat down across from her at the island. "Look, Cat, I've been gone a whole year, and we all know how my happily ever after turned out. But through all this, I've learned one thing, and it's that honesty is the keystone of any relationship. If you don't have that, you don't have anything. And you know what? The honesty part starts with yourself."

"I'm not sure what you're talking about."

"I'm saying that before you walk away, don't be afraid to demand honesty of him and of yourself. Then if it doesn't work, you have nothing to look back on with regret."

Liz wrapped her arms around her and gave her a kiss on the head. "I'm glad you're back," Cat whispered.

"Me, too," she said.

Cat waited until Liz left and she was alone in the kitchen, the muffled sounds of chatter and laughter from outside filtering through the glass doors. God, would this day never end? She really did have a splitting headache. Now that Brady knew Preston and she weren't dating, he wasn't shy at all about letting her know his interest. Despite Preston's conviction in telling her good-bye for good, he had seemed agitated and tense.

All she knew was she'd had it with men, and she needed some Advil stat. She headed from the kitchen to the bathroom, which was off the front hall. On the way, she noticed a wallet and phone sitting next to her keys where she'd placed them on the polished antique hall table her mother kept underneath the arch of the staircase.

Preston's. They were still sitting there from when he'd stopped to give Nick the business card. A family portrait taken when she was sixteen sat above the table. Life had seemed so simple then. She glanced from her newly-without-braces smile down to the objects on the table.

Lacey's voice sounded in her head again. *If you don't believe me, check his wallet.*

Cat wasn't a snoop. She'd never read her sisters' diaries or flipped through their desk drawers.

What was it Liz had just said? That honesty was the cornerstone of any relationship. Had Preston's pride trumped his ability to be honest? He was a proud man who hated to show weakness of any kind. Opening that wallet could be a once-in-a-lifetime opportunity, one she was certain would never come again. If there was a chance something in there could explain the contradiction between his feelings and his actions, she was going to take it.

Her hand hovered over the wallet. The flip side was that it could lead to more disappointment when she found nothing amiss. Besides, if there had ever been anything in his wallet having to do with her, it had likely been removed long ago.

But still.

With trembling hands, she lifted the smooth soft leather square, turned it over in her palm, noted its slightly worn edges. The public part of Preston always was so perfectly put together, the thought that his wallet was a little rough around the edges made her smile. A noise made her jump and almost drop it—the tumble of ice cubes from the ice maker into the bin in the freezer. She had to act fast. So she opened it.

Her eyes scanned quickly over the typical male wallet contents. Credit cards, a ticket stub, his driver's license. Nothing spectacular. She was just berating herself for violating his privacy when something caught her eye. Tucked behind a sales receipt in a clear plastic window was a photo. With trembling fingers, she pulled it up enough so she could see it.

It was a photo of her from last September, taken at a wedding of two high school friends. She was dressed in a strapless cream-colored silk dress, holding a clutch, and grinning widely for the camera, the concrete steps of the church behind her. She'd just walked out of the church and was about to join the crowd to wait for the bride and groom.

She barely remembered it being taken. Preston had captured her at a perfect moment—caught up in the joy of the wedding, forgetting the fact that she'd come without a date— she'd tagged along with Derrick and Jenna. Still upset over her recent breakup, she hadn't wanted to be seen, to be confronted by well-meaning friends, but she'd forced herself to go, and the day had turned out to be unexpectedly fun. Preston had been snapping pictures all day using his fancy new camera lens, and he'd been joking with her, teasing her. What had he said? *Hey, beautiful, turn and smile for the camera.*

That last night before he deployed, they'd walked out together from the wedding. They'd been dancing, every single dance. He'd walked her to his car. There under the full moon, the moonlight casting bluish ethereal beams through the magnolia branches overhead, he took hold of both her hands and pulled her up from where she was leaning against the car, up, up, and into his strong arms. And then he kissed her. A spectacular, magical kiss that began featherlight and breezy and turned into something completely different. He slid his hand around the nape of her bare neck and pulled her against him, and she'd clutched at his back, feeling the taut planes of muscle, the strength, the soft, wonderful feel of his lips on hers.

Their lips met, at first tentatively, and then suddenly joining with a hunger she'd never known. At the time, she'd attributed it to the relief of finally letting go of Robert. And the champagne, and the fact that she hadn't had sex since a month before she and Robert had broken up.

She'd wanted to taste every part of him, and she opened her mouth and welcomed his tongue, met it with her own and pressed herself against his rock-hard body.

She tugged at the lapels of his tux. "Take me to your hotel," she said boldly. His new house on the lake wasn't even finished being framed yet, she couldn't offer to bring him back to her parents' place, and time was short. He was leaving at 5:00 a.m. for the airport, and she didn't want to spend another minute tiptoeing around how much she wanted to be with him.

He kissed her again, hard, and she ran her hands down the densely corded muscles of his back. She felt free, freer than she had since Robert had bailed nearly two months earlier.

Preston pulled away, holding her at arm's length. Stroked her cheek with one finger. His touch was so gentle, just like the look in his eyes. She didn't want the fairy tale to end. For her dress to turn to rags and for him to be gone, thousands of miles away, when they'd finally found each other.

She reached up and grasped his arms. "Let's not waste any more time," she said, tugging on him.

"I-I can't, Cat."

"You—don't want me?"

"More than anything, but not like this."

"I haven't had that much to drink," she said.

"It's not that. It's too soon. I don't want to be your rebound."

"You're not my rebound," she'd said. A part of her had loved him forever, and being with him now seemed like the most natural—and the most brazen—thing she'd ever done. She wanted to tell him it didn't have anything to do with the strange spell a wedding casts, that it went far deeper than that.

There was something else, too. She didn't want to admit she was afraid for him. That she wanted him now, before he left, because God only knew what lay ahead of them.

He leaned his forehead against hers. She felt the warmth of his skin, the heaviness of his breath striking her cheek. "Your brother is my lifelong friend, and I have to honor my bond to him. Doing a one-nighter with you and then leaving— it's not right." He kissed her forehead, her cheeks. Tipped her chin up until she looked at him and said, his voice cracking, "You're so beautiful. I want to always remember you like this, how you are tonight, and what a perfect day this was." He'd raised her hands to his lips and kissed every knuckle, slowly, one at a time, which sent shivers coursing up her spine. Then he'd helped her into the car.

In her parents' hallway, Cat slipped the photo back down behind the receipt and replaced the wallet. She swiped at the tears that rolled freely down her cheeks.

She didn't know why he still carried her photograph, but judging from its front and center position, it must have been a conscious decision. Preston was a complicated man who was courageous and brave and wounded. If left to his own devices, he'd shut her out forever, thinking it was for her own good.

She didn't believe in fairy tales anymore. Her own had ended over a year ago, and she was smarter and wiser for it. She'd never been a risk taker, had never had a one-night stand, or even slept with another guy besides Robert, whom she'd met in college. She'd led her whole life by the book, and what had it gotten her? A job she was unhappy with and a near miss with a guy who was safe, boring, and completely wrong for her.

Maybe Preston was right. That she did secretly crave risk. That she longed to be released from the confines of convention she'd built so carefully around her own life. Choosing the most logical fiancé, the most logical job. Maybe it was time to cut the strings of everyone's expectations about her and free-fall for once in her life.

Preston would never offer her a wounded version of himself. That was the kind of guy he was. Proud to a fault, and stubborn as a little boy's cowlick.

She was going to bring him down.

Operation Take Down Preston was going to start bright and early.

Chapter Twelve

Preston waited for Cat in the lobby of the Lake Watchacatchee Lodge, leaning against one of the rustic wooden columns and watching Friday afternoon visitors roll their luggage to the reservation desk, happy and excited for a relaxing weekend at the popular getaway. When he was a teenager, in addition to his job at the shoe store, he used to be a bellhop and a busboy in the restaurant here. He'd taken all the extra hours he could to avoid being home and to make all the money he could. Sometimes he'd even slept on the couch in the supervisor's office and showered in a vacated guest room before reporting to work the next day.

He flexed and released his shoulders, hoping to shake off the black shadows of his past. Part of him wished he could stay in the comfort of his own lake house—alone, and away from the stares of well-meaning people—but this weekend was his obligation to Nick as his best man, and he'd fulfill it to the best of his ability. Cat and he had both agreed to put their personal feelings aside and just get through the weekend for Maddie and Nick's sakes.

He looked up to see Cat walking down the wide central staircase wearing a colorful beach cover-up, flip-flops, and sunglasses atop her head. She carried a bright orange beach bag slung over her shoulder. Her fresh beauty and wide smile made several men's heads turn in the lobby. On instinct, he picked up his pace and joined her as she reached the bottom of the stairs.

"We're the first ones here. Ready to get some sun?" she asked.

He wouldn't give a rat's ass if it were storming out, because she was all the sun he would ever need, standing right in front of him. The thought of spending time with her alone both thrilled and terrified. He weighed the decision before him. This would be his last chance to confess everything before the wedding weekend got into full swing. Tell her exactly what he thought of Brady, and tell her the truth about why he let her go.

He broke out in a cold sweat. Usually he was decisive, always knew the right course. But as far as Cat was concerned, he seemed to have lost his compass.

"Are you ready?" She linked her arm with his. She smelled of suntan lotion and some pretty, citrusy scent that made him want to gather her up and inhale big gulps of her freshness. "I can't remember the last time I've just laid out and had a lazy afternoon," she said.

He couldn't, either. He usually detested lying around, sitting still, doing nothing. But somehow, just the thought of sitting next to her at the beach made his pulse quicken.

He offered to help her carry her load, but she said she was fine. He turned all his focus on walking, lest he trip and make an ass of himself. He made it through the lobby without too much lumbering and out on the wooden boardwalk that led to the beach. She grabbed a beach umbrella from a stack. "Let me take that," he said, insisting, tugging on it. To his surprise, she resisted. They stood there about to get into a tug-of-war over it.

She lifted her sunglasses onto her head. "You have to learn that just for now, your priority is healing yourself. Okay?" The emerald depths of her eyes showed compassion, not pity. Her voice was gentle. Both of them made him relent.

"Okay," he said, surrendering his hold. "You carry it down for us."

He lagged behind as she walked, then she suddenly turned around. "And don't think you're carrying beach chairs, either." She knew him too well. "I thought we could just lay out on our towels. Would that be comfortable for you?"

He nodded. Something was different about her, but he couldn't quite put his finger on it. Maybe it was her decisive tone, or an attitude he sensed that told him she wasn't going to take any bullshit.

They walked together to an open spot on the sand. She took his towel and unrolled it for him, and he let her, enjoying watching how she moved, how she insisted on taking charge, and somehow, he liked it. He liked being here with her, just the two of them. The desperate yearning he always felt for her seemed to be in check, held back by her attention and concern. For the hundredth time, he told himself he was doing the right thing to not tell her the full story.

He insisted on planting their umbrella, despite her protests, and he had the task done in no time. They decided to lie in the sun first, and use the umbrella for shade when they got too hot. He knew Cat didn't tan very well, and she was already spraying lots of SPF 50 all over her legs.

"Don't sit down yet," she said.

"Why not?" In answer, she walked over and began spraying his back with the suntan stuff. "I'm okay," he mumbled, until she began rubbing the lotion in. Her hands felt so damn good on his skin as she ran them gently along his back. Each touch felt like little shocks of fire, and he was burning up under her kind, cool touch. His breath came heavy, and he became too choked up to even thank her.

She seemed unaffected. She handed him the can. "Would you do my back, please?" Before he could answer, she lifted her cover-up and in one swoop, tossed it off and to the ground.

He swallowed. Gulped hard. Tried to keep his eyes from bugging out of his head. Because in front of him was the most gorgeous woman he'd ever seen, wearing the tiniest bikini on the planet.

"Do you like it?" she asked with the excitement of a little girl twirling in a new dress rather than a woman in a barely-there bathing suit, a little green polka-dot number barely held together by some flimsy ties.

"I-um-yeah." Great, his hormones had reduced him to the pre-linguistic skills of a caveman. He focused on shaking the can instead of talking.

Then she turned around and oh, Lordy, gave him the rear view. She lifted her arms to gather up her hair and twist it into a ponytail. Which allowed him to see all along the curve of her beautiful arched back and her sweet ass, which was barely covered by a skinny scrap of material. He was not going to survive this day much less the next hour.

He sprayed but didn't dare touch her. She turned her face, pointing to her back. "If you can, just rub it in a little over my shoulders and the middle of my back. So I don't burn. Please."

She sounded so innocent, but he wondered if she was playing with him. Flaunting all her amazing curves and those miles of soft skin, breaking him down.

"Cat, I—"

"Hurry, in case clouds roll in."

Fat chance. The sky was a brilliant aquamarine blue, and the only trace of a cloud was the snowy trail of a jetliner that had sliced through it like a skywriter.

Somehow, he rubbed in a bit of the spray. He got though it as quickly as possible, trying not to notice how soft and warm and pliant her skin was under his fingers. And how much he wanted to kiss the back of her long, graceful neck, maybe even bite down playfully on the curve of her shoulder. Everything about her was amazing. Even her quirks, like making certain every square inch of her skin was covered with sunscreen. He had to look away when she sprayed under the skimpy strings that held the sides of her suit bottoms together. How could that bastard Robert have given away such a gem?

She collapsed onto her towel and spread his out evenly where the breeze had rolled the edge over. Then she patted it and looked up at him with a grin. "All ready for you, partner."

He lumbered down in his awkward way, good leg first, arms supporting his weight as he carefully lowered the bad leg. Cat looked at the brace. While he hated her seeing him like this, he felt only her usual matter-of-fact concern as she asked, "How's the leg?"

"My therapist says it's looking a little less gnarly than last week. She made me see that the doctor's report wasn't that bad." He just had to stick to his routine, keep doing his exercises, and not stress his leg. All of which he'd do religiously, because that word "normal" was a dream he wanted almost as desperately as he wanted Cat.

"Oh, Preston. That's great." She flashed him a big smile, then lay back and closed her eyes, pulling her sunglasses over her eyes. "It's a perfect day. Sort of makes you forget your other troubles, you know?"

He lay next to her and felt the sun penetrate his skin. The breeze stirred. Gulls cried overhead, kids laughed, and somebody's radio played a Bruno Mars tune in the background. He smiled a little, feeling the first bits of tightness loosen up inside him. She was right. Staying in the moment, with her, was a balm to his soul. Until something made him open his eyes. She was leaning over him.

He startled. "What are you doing? You scared the hell out of me." Then he realized what a great view of her chest he suddenly had, which made him ache to slide his hand under the tiny bit of material covering her breasts and touch her soft flesh. Plus she'd tipped forward against him a little, the velvety skin of her midriff touching his side. He frowned.

She lifted up her sunglasses. "Life is good, Preston. It's still mostly good."

He laughed out loud. "Thank you, Little Miss Sunshine. Yeah, sometimes life is still good." What was she doing to him? His heart was hammering in his chest; he was alert and on edge, and horny as hell.

She flopped back down on her towel and closed her eyes.

He couldn't help looking at her. She was all lean curves, pretty legs, and bright blue toenails. And—what the hell? Her belly button had a ring in it.

A ring. Prim, proper, Catherine Kingston had a belly button ring. That realization must have short-circuited his brain, because before he knew what he was doing, he'd touched it. Her abdominal muscles tensed when his fingers grazed her abdomen, and her stomach went hollow with her sudden intake of breath. She went still and turned her head toward him.

Somehow his entire body froze in place. He was totally transfixed by the feel of her beneath his hand. "W-what is that?" he managed to say.

She placed her small hand over his large one. Her pale skin was a huge contrast to his naturally darker tone. "A belly button ring, and don't act like you've never seen one."

"I have. Just not on you."

"You don't like it?" she asked, still not moving her hand.

"No, I-I like it. Just surprised is all."

"I could surprise you about a lot of things," she said. He

looked at her in alarm. Was she flirting with him, or about to tell him off? Her sunglasses were too dark, and he couldn't read the expression in her eyes.

"You always surprise me," he said.

"How's that?" she asked.

She'd surprised him during those first few months in Afghanistan, when she'd always been there for him, sending him letters and crazy things in care packages. Like pens with pink feathers and her romance novels with pages of love scenes marked and little sticky notes that said, "Read this! And think of me." She'd sent him crazy patterned socks and gum and instant Starbucks coffee that was as close to being fresh-ground as it could get. She'd been open and honest and giving, and she still was, regardless of how shitty he'd treated her. And that was the most surprising thing of all—her inability to give him up.

"You stood up to your family the other night," he said. "Life's too short to not do what you want."

She sat up suddenly, and his hand fell to his side. "If you mean that, really mean that, what is it that *you* want?"

"Cat, I—"

"No." She put a hand on his arm. "Tell me, Preston, what is it that you want? Because you could have it. You could have all of it just for the asking."

Blood pounded in his ears. Had he heard her right? She was offering herself up, not to Brady, but to *him*. And he wanted her, every blessed part of her. He wanted to run his hands all along her smooth, sun-warmed body. He wanted to peel off those scraps of what she called a bathing suit and explore every part of her. With his tongue. Including that belly button ring.

She lifted his hand from where it lay at his side and intertwined their fingers. "No matter how much you try to deny it, we just fit."

God, he loved the feel of her. He closed his eyes, reveling in the sensations that only existed in his imagination day after day for far too long. All this time without her, all those months of denial…all those secret little things they'd whispered and emailed and wrote…months of foreplay…and now to have her right beside him. Half naked. It was plain torture. Without thinking, he brought their joined hands to his lips and kissed hers, holding on tight. A little too tight, the way a desperate man grips a lifeline to stop himself from falling off a cliff. On impulse, he placed her hand on his chest, over his heart, and put his on top.

"Don't talk," she whispered. "Just—be with me." She lifted her sunglasses so he could see everything that was in her eyes. See *her*.

As soon as he looked into those bright green eyes, he knew she'd worn him down. He could no longer hide his confusion or his absolute need. He had so much to say, but she'd somehow given him permission to forget all of it for these few moments of heaven. Then somehow he did let go—of all his thoughts, his worries, and all his unspoken confessions. Forgot about his broken body and his broken spirit and simply enjoyed these few precious moments on a hot, perfect day under a warm sun with the one woman he wanted more than anything.

They lay like that for he didn't know how long. He focused on the feel of her, her small hand, searing a path into his heart, his soul, and willed himself to stay in the moment. Inhaled the fresh lake air and absorbed the warmth of the sun and tried to let a peace settle over him. But his heart wouldn't calm—his pulse had skyrocketed faster than a Tesla on the open road, and he was certain she felt every beat louder than a bongo drum. He couldn't let go, couldn't move, as if he was desperate to make these few brief moments stretch out for an eternity.

"Preston." Her soft breath tickled his cheek. The sound of his name was low and a little throaty, and he suddenly knew she was as turned on as he was. When he finally had the courage to force his gaze from the perfect summer sky to look at her, he thought he saw the same desperate wanting that reverberated clear through his very marrow. Mindlessly, he reached his other hand up to hook a wayward strand of hair behind her ear. His gaze dropped to her mouth. Her lips were full and soft, and all it would take was one quick movement—

"Hey, you two," a voice from behind them said, breaking the spell. Preston lifted his hand off hers and sat up on his elbows.

Brady walked up to them dressed in navy swim trunks and no shirt, flashing a grin that made Preston want to squeeze all his whitening toothpaste clear out of its tube.

"Oh, hi, Brady," Cat said, sitting up.

"How long have you been out here?" he asked, his gaze traveling over every inch of Cat in a predatory way he didn't bother to hide.

Not long enough, Preston thought, already missing the feel of her. Every instinct he possessed went on guard, prepared to claim her as his own. He wondered if Brady suspected something was going on between them, maybe had even purposefully interrupted them.

"Not long," Cat said. "We were enjoying the beautiful day."

"It is at that," Brady said, still not taking his eyes off her. To Preston's dismay, he spread his towel on the other side of Cat and stretched out, putting his hands behind his head and looking out over the lake. Preston noted how rock-hard his abs were, how he seemed to be intentionally positioning himself, flexing his muscles so Cat could admire them. Preston half expected Brady to get up and start doing bodybuilding poses.

"So, Cat, how's the maid of honor? All your duties fulfilled? Because if they are, maybe you'd like to go for a walk with me?" Then he turned to Preston "Pres, you wouldn't mind if we went for a little walk together, would you? A few of us are going to have a little race later. We can walk down and see my canoe."

Right. He was going to show her his canoe. Now he'd heard everything.

Over his dead body.

"You could come, too, Preston," Brady said, then released an exaggerated sigh. "Oh, sorry. I forgot. I wouldn't want to do anything to aggravate your injury." His gaze lingered on Preston's bum leg.

"I assure you, Brady, there's nothing wrong with my upper body strength." Preston couldn't resist flexing his pecs a little. "I'd be happy to take part in a little friendly athletic competition."

"You mean like chess, Trivial Pursuit? Those might be safer options."

Preston grinned widely. "Funny. Where do you race to?"

"From the dock on this side across the lake and back. There're a couple canoes down there we can use."

"I'm up for it. Unless you're a little frightened of some real competition. I mean, I wouldn't want to embarrass you."

Brady grinned. "You're on."

Cat shot Preston a you-must-be-crazy look, but he gave her a wink. "I'll meet you down there," Preston said to Brady, who immediately stood up from the sand and started jogging toward the dock. Preston hoisted himself up as gracefully as he could in front of Cat, gave her another wink, and followed Brady across the sand and down the grassy hill.

Suddenly, he felt the waistband of his bathing suit snap. He turned to see Cat behind him, standing planted with her arms on her hips, looking pissed. "What do you think you're doing?" she asked.

"Just a friendly competition among men," he said a little

sheepishly.

"What do you think you're trying to prove?" She was all big green eyes and concern, and his heart swelled from seeing it.

"Why, sweetheart, are you worried about me? Don't be, because I'll be fine." He flexed his biceps. "Nothing's wrong with the guns." What *was* he trying to prove? All he knew was as soon as Brady started moving in on Cat, he'd clicked into warrior mode, and it was strangely exhilarating.

"You don't have to prove anything. To him or to me. Plus, it's not worth it to jeopardize your leg."

Common sense told him she was right. But his testosterone had flared, and all he wanted to do was beat the crap out of this guy—figuratively speaking, of course. Mostly.

"I know that." But he had to prove something to himself. No force on earth was going to allow this guy to move in on his woman.

His woman. Before he could figure out what the hell that meant, he'd stepped forward and kissed her. Right on those soft sun-warmed lips, pleased when she made a soft gasp at the contact. Then he turned and headed down to the lake.

• • •

Cat touched her fingers to her lips, which still tingled from where Preston had just kissed her. She watched the two men head down to the lake, Brady's confident gait alongside Preston's ungainly one. Something had shifted between him and her. She felt it, and she knew he did, too. So why had he egged Brady on like this? It couldn't end well.

"What's going on?" Cat looked up to see Maddie walking down the hill toward her, accompanied by Jenna and Liz. She joined them in walking the rest of the way to the lake.

"Preston and Brady are racing like two little kids," Cat

said.

"Why?" Jenna asked.

"Uh-oh," Liz said. "It's a testosterone contest, isn't it? One that began at our house over dinner the other night."

"Preston's showing off for you, Cat," Maddie said. "He's being territorial. That's really sweet."

Cat rolled her eyes. She had no idea what was going through Preston's mind, only that it was foolish and unnecessary, and as soon as he made it back to dry land, she was going to tell him so, again. Nick and Derrick had gathered near the dock to be closer to the action and were laughing and shouting about rules and directions. Someone whistled loudly, and the boats took off.

"I think Preston actually has a chance to beat that guy," Liz said, squinting into the sun as the two men paddled furiously up the lake. "He's strong."

And an incredible chest, Cat noted, which was on display for everyone to see and admire in all its muscular glory. Yep, there was nothing wrong with that glistening set of pectorals, no sirree.

"This is the first time I've seen the old Preston back," Derrick said.

"What's gotten into him?" Nick asked. "He's rowing like there's a lot more at stake than a beer."

Maybe there was. Cat knew about the relentless chin-ups, bench presses, weights, and other exercises Preston had been doing double-time to work out his upper body since the injury. Then she remembered something else. "It also doesn't hurt that he crewed at West Point."

Watching him in the boat was like watching a warrior in action. Brady gave a gallant try, but it was nothing like the no-holds-barred, 250 percent effort that Preston put into every stroke as if his life depended on it.

Things got crazy on the home stretch. Brady flung water

from his oar into Preston's boat. Preston laughed and used his oar to flick some water right back. Preston won by two boat lengths. Both men got out of their boats dripping wet and laughing. Nick handed them each a beer, Derrick patted them on the back, and they walked up the hill laughing and trash-talking each other.

Preston stopped when they neared Cat. "I won," he said grinning like a five-year-old.

"Nice race," Brady said. "You got lucky. I want a rematch tomorrow."

"Not a chance, I won fair and square. You'll just have to go cry into your beer."

"Yeah, the round you buy," Brady said. "See you at dinner." The two men parted with a shake.

Cat waited for Preston to walk the short way to meet her while the others went ahead to change for dinner.

He was dripping wet. She opened her mouth to tell him how silly or unnecessary all this was, but she stopped in her tracks. Pure masculine power radiated from him, from the dragon that spread itself across his broad chest to his powerful build, not at all diminished by his limp. He was smiling like he'd just won a state championship. Triumphant. So she shook her head and grinned back. He glanced at the incline before them before turning his gaze on Cat. "Mind if I lean on you a little up the hill?" he asked.

She stopped for a minute and stared at him. His eyes were that same piercing color as always, matching the glorious blue sky. But the shadows had lifted, and what she saw there took her breath away. "Could you possibly be asking me for—help?"

"Just a little," he said, his face flushing a little as he squinted into the distance.

She flew into his arms and wrapped her arms tightly around his lean waist. Rested her cheek against the clean-smelling T-shirt he'd just shrugged on. His arm came to rest on the small of her back, at first tentative, then stronger. For a moment she stood like that, touching him, the rest of the world fading away in the hot afternoon sunshine.

"Hey, you two, not to interrupt your moment, but we'll meet you at the lodge for dinner," Nick called.

Preston looked up and gave a wave, then gently held Cat at arm's length. "If I would have known I'd get that reaction, I would have asked for help a long time ago."

"I can't help it if you're a slow learner, Guthrie," Cat said, pulling his arm around her shoulder so he could lean on her as they headed up the hill.

Chapter Thirteen

"Why are you not nervous?" Preston asked Nick the next afternoon in the side room off the front of the church as he helped him straighten his tie. They were alone for a few rare moments before the other groomsmen would join them before the wedding. "You're making my job as best man too easy."

Nick laughed. "When it's right, it's right."

"Seriously?" Preston asked. "You can't do better than that?"

"Look, remember those days when we used to hang out and chase women?"

"Very well, thanks."

"Well, those were fun times, but they are nothing compared to the experience of really loving the right person." He grinned widely. "One day, buddy, you're going to experience it, too."

Preston snorted to be manly, but a piece of him did have a tiny inkling of what he was talking about. His heart knew what his brain couldn't quite put together. And that scared the shit out of him.

"I know about your fake dating arrangement with Cat." Preston started to respond, but Nick cut him off. "Maddie told me. But I also know how much you care about her. I never thought it would happen to me, Pres, but it did. All I can say is, when it hits you, it hits you hard, and there's no stopping it. You may as well give up the fight, because it's gonna get you no matter what you do. Whether you think you deserve it or not. Whether you're afraid of it or not. My advice is don't fight it."

Preston smiled at his friend. Derrick may have been the friend he shared his youth with, but Nick was his partner and his confidante. "I never thought I'd see the day," Preston said, shaking his head in mock sadness. "But it couldn't have happened to a nicer person. Or a better friend."

"Life surprises you," Nick said, putting his hand on Preston's shoulder. "Wait and see."

Preston never attended a single wedding as a kid. His family had been too dysfunctional. But the entire ceremony, all its pomp and tradition, fascinated him and made him unexpectedly emotional. Nick could not take his eyes off Maddie as she came up the aisle looking radiant on her father's and mother's arms. The couple's love for each other was palpable. The love of their families was, too.

He thought that was intense, but nothing prepared him for seeing Cat dressed in a pale pink gown, carrying a bouquet of some bright pink and white flowers and wearing a few of them in her hair. He kept sneaking glimpses of her, and she kept catching him like they were teenagers with a crush on each other. When it was all over and he walked her down the aisle, he wanted to kiss her just from the sheer joy he felt at being with her and being a part of this special day for their friends. He walked a little slowly, but she didn't seem to mind.

Just for today he thought he'd take Nick's advice. Stop

fighting and simply be with Cat and allow himself to be swept away by her beauty, her sense of fun, and her goodness. Let it wash all over him like rain to a man whose body and soul were parched. Just for today, he'd allow himself to take all she had to offer. Whether he deserved it or not.

. . .

Payback was a bitch. Preston was sitting at the table in the lodge restaurant during the reception drumming his fingers and watching that ass Brady dance with the women. Actually, the fact that he was dancing with Jenna and Maddie and Cat didn't bother him in the slightest. They were all out there having fun, and he had no problem with that. It was when the tempo slowed and the lights dimmed and he drew nearer to Cat that Preston's blood pressure cranked up to boiling.

"You do realize that what you're about to do impacts me, don't you?" Liz took a sip of wine, then leveled her gaze at him.

"Beg your pardon?" he asked. He and Liz were the only ones sitting, and he was in no mood for small talk. He had a mission to complete, and he had to act fast.

"Once you break them up, that guy is going to come over here and ask me to dance."

"Is that a bad thing?"

"Look, I can be as moody and brooding as you, Guthrie, okay? It's bad enough to sit here and smile pretty while I watch everyone couple off."

Preston smiled. "Tell me about it."

"Unfortunately, I'm his second choice, and I don't like to be second best at anything."

"So tell him no."

"I'd love to, but I'll do anything to help my sister. If that means I've got to keep him preoccupied for a little while so

he leaves her alone, I'll do it. Speaking of Cat, one little issue."
She set down her glass and lowered her voice. "If you hurt her
again, I'll make certain your good leg doesn't work, either."

"Thanks, Liz." He shot her a wide smile. "Being as you're
a doctor, I'll take that under advisement. And I appreciate
your sacrifice. But now I've got to go."

He stood up a little too fast and had to grab on to the
table for support. Pain shot through his leg, and he had to
breathe deep and let it pass. All the walking he'd been doing
this weekend was catching up to him, and that trek up the
hill yesterday after the canoe race had cost him. Well, he'd
slow down after today. When he saw Brady slip a hand around
Cat's waist, he knew he couldn't wait another second.

"Hey, buddy, don't you think you should be resting that
leg?" Brady said with a lazy grin as Preston approached.
Preston wasn't amused. It had taken all of two seconds for
this guy to become a complete pain in the ass again.

Preston wanted to tell him he thought he should be resting
his *mouth*, but he refrained. "You've had a hard weekend,
losing that rowing race and all. Let me cut in and dance with
Cat, okay?"

Brady narrowed down his gaze. "You're a little bit touchy
for someone in a fake relationship, aren't you?"

Preston laughed. An artificial, phony laugh that sounded
scary even to his own ears. "Um, about that fake relationship.
Turns out that it's not so fake." He turned to Cat. "May I have
this dance?"

Cat looked from Brady to him. Even in the dim light, he
could see that her cheeks flushed, and that was a great relief
to him. He prayed that she still wanted him as badly as he
wanted her.

He wanted her with an ache that was worse than all the
physical pain he'd endured since his return. Worse than all his
mental anguish, and the fears that he was not a whole man

and never would be again. Wanting her was larger than that, all of it.

"Thanks for the dances, Brady," Cat said. "But if you don't mind, I'm going to dance with Preston now."

"Okay," Brady said with an exaggerated sigh. "When he has to sit down and rest, come find me."

The bastard had the audacity to wink at Cat. As he walked off, Preston couldn't help scowling at his parting barb. He must have done a bad job at hiding his intense dislike and the fact that he was ready to have it out with him, because Cat reached up and smoothed the lines between his eyes. Her fingers were cool, and her touch made some of his tension dissipate.

Brady wasn't worth wasting his time on. Not when he had *her* in his arms.

"Do you have a fever or something?" Cat asked as he took up her hand in his and curled it against his chest, pulling her close to him and wrapping his other hand around her waist. "Because you're acting a little strange."

He tightened his grip on her waist until he'd pulled her tight against his body, until her breasts grazed his chest and their hips made contact. He was certain—and pleased—that she could feel the evidence of how much he wanted her. Her scent—powder fresh and clean, flowery or something, made him want to inhale it, and her, in big gulps.

He shot her a long, slow grin. "Yeah. I guess I am. The only cure for whatever I've got is you."

She shot him a puzzled look, but her mouth turned up in a smile. They were so close, he could feel her sigh as she surrendered to the feeling, curling in closer to him and swaying gently to the music.

"I'm sorry I can't move very much," he said in a low voice. "I may never be able to dance again like Brady does. I can barely manage to shuffle."

"Who says we have to move at all?" She smiled at him. Her eyes were lit up and focused solely on him, too, in that way she had that made a man want to tell her all his secrets. But now wasn't the time.

He bent his head and kissed her. She responded by melting against him and wrapping her arms around his neck. Her lips met his, parting on a sigh, and he wasted no time in cupping his hand gently around her neck, pulling her even closer, and entwining his tongue with hers. He couldn't get enough of her sweet taste. He pulled back just enough to speak, to tell her he was taking her to bed without passing Go, but he was interrupted by a tap on his shoulder.

The song ended, and one with a new, faster tempo was beginning. Preston turned to find Brady at his back, grinning that blinding smile. "My turn now, Guthrie. Time to give it a rest."

Did this guy not get the message? Preston was about to tell him off when he saw that Maddie and Nick were herding everyone into a line, laughing and beckoning for everyone to join in on the Electric Slide. Liz was back on the dance floor, and Jenna and Derrick, too; even the Kingston parents and grandparents. Preston reluctantly let go of Cat's hand. She looked at him with a question in her eyes. He bent close to her ear and said, "We'll finish this later." She only had time to nod before Brady grabbed her hand and swept her into the line. Preston bowed out, walking to the sidelines to watch the entire family having fun.

Brady was a great dancer. Good-looking, great moves. There wasn't much about him that wasn't perfect for the job or for Cat except for Preston's jealousy.

It wasn't just Brady that bothered him. He'd suddenly gotten reminded of more of what he was lacking in—a family. The give-and-take, the joking, the goofing around, it was all foreign to him. He suddenly felt a need for air, so he left the reception hall, leaving the dancing to those with two working legs.

. . .

Cat saw the moment Preston left the restaurant and walked out onto the expansive covered porch that overlooked the big hill leading down to the lake. As soon as she'd done her duty for Maddie and Nick and could extract herself from Brady's grip, she went outside and scanned the porch. Its outdoor tables were full of laughing, chatting people. No Preston in sight.

She hadn't imagined those kisses, or the look in his eyes that she'd been dreaming of for the past year. If she had to search every blessed acre of the lakefront to find him, she would. She vowed that they were going to finish this tonight, one way or another.

A bright white line carved the sky, followed by an ominous crack of thunder. The humidity was about a thousand percent, so it was no surprise that a storm was on the horizon.

The dewy grass tickled her toes as she walked down the hill in her sandals, carefully lifting the hem of her gown. The night was balmy, and the crickets and locusts were competing with each other for who could sing the loudest. Then she saw him in the shadows, his broad shoulders hunched over the dock railing, looking out over the lake.

More like brooding, but she wasn't going to allow that.

She was going to be bold and risky and put herself on the line. Preston had been right when he'd said some part of her *was* bold. Bold or just plain desperate, she wasn't sure. Maybe it was the deep-in-her-soul need to fight for a man she simply could not give up on.

"There you are," she said. "Why'd you run off?"

He stood up, the corded muscles of his back tense

beneath his shirt. He placed his cell phone into his pocket. "I was wishing my brother a happy birthday. And doing some thinking," he said.

She rolled her eyes. "Thinking or reconsidering?"

That caught his attention. He turned around, frowning.

She tossed up her hands in exasperation. "I don't want to dance with Brady. I don't like Brady. I like you."

"I know that."

"Oh. So you're not jealous?"

"Yes, I'm jealous, dammit," he said. "That's not the issue. My feelings—"

"Don't matter because you came back wounded? Should be shut off because you're having some problems?" She snorted, and a big fat raindrop plopped on her back. Followed by another and another.

"We should head back up to the lodge."

He was so damn…impassive. His face was a wall of thick safety glass, and she had no idea how to put a crack in it.

She poked him again. "I don't want to go anywhere. I want to talk to you—really talk. I want you to stop using dumb excuses like Brady to push me away."

He put his hands on her arms and looked at her. This time, there was no mistaking the conflict in his eyes. The crack she was looking for. "I've tried to make you understand that it would be a lot better for you to leave. So help me, Cat, you've got to turn around and walk up that hill without me, or you'll regret it."

"Regret what? That I want you? I'm an adult now. I'm not Derrick's baby sister anymore."

"I came back messed up, and I'm not just talking about my leg. You deserve more than to get saddled with my problems. Please, I'm begging you, just turn around and leave."

Splat, splat, splat. Messy droplets pinged on the trees overhead.

She crossed her arms. "I'm not leaving."

Lightning sizzled through the sky and thunder cracked. Preston took her arm and pulled her along the field toward the gazebo. "Run ahead. I'll meet you in the shelter."

She shook her head. "I'm staying with you. Whether we get wet or not, you're stuck with me."

Halfway across the field, the rain let loose, dousing them with sheets of cool water. Cat took off her shoes and ran barefoot the last remaining distance to the gazebo. By the time they reached it, they were soaked and out of breath.

Preston leaned up against the whitewashed railing. In the dim light cast from the lodge on the hill before them, she could see the strong features of his face—the squarely set jaw, the determined set of his mouth. The fight in his eyes. She moved closer, but he held his hand up.

"If you touch me again, I can't promise to be in control of my behavior."

She laughed.

"I wasn't being funny."

"It's a little funny." She inched closer.

He shook his head. "Cat, please. I don't want to—"

She wrapped her wet arms around his waist. Looked into his eyes. He was a big guy, a warrior, all brawn and hardness. A man who was so severely hard on himself that he couldn't even see it, but she swore she saw a glimmer of his marshmallow insides.

His posture was rigid, his thick brows pulled down in a frown, but he didn't back away from her touch.

Good, because this time, she wasn't giving up. "I lost a fiancé and a job, and I walked out of my only job interview. And I'm living with my parents. If we wait for life to be perfect, we'll be waiting forever."

She acted on impulse to cup his cheek and didn't miss the brief wince he made at her touch. She touched him anyway, running her fingers along the roughness of his five-o'clock shadow, enjoying the contrast between smooth and rough. Stubborn and soft. Holding the line and giving in. She was determined to make him cave.

"I'm damaged," he blurted. "I've never felt my faults like I do since I've been back. I-I don't know what I can offer you. All I know is I want to wrap my hands around that guy's neck every time he touches you."

"Take me home," she said softly, standing on tiptoe and placing her lips against his ear. "Make love to me, Preston. Do it because you're an honorable man, and it's the right thing to do."

His grip on her arms tightened, and his eyes lit up with agonized feeling. "So help me God, Cat. I've tried but I can't stay away." With one quick movement, he pulled her to him, his lips crushing hers, his tongue sweeping inside her mouth in strokes of hot, pure pleasure. He pulled back long enough to murmur against her lips, "Let's get out of here."

Chapter Fourteen

As they crossed the threshold of his house, Preston kicked the front door shut behind them with his foot, not wanting to let go of Cat for even a second. They were out of breath and sopping wet. Cat gave an involuntary shiver as the air-conditioning hit her wet skin.

"Are you cold?" he asked, running his hands up and down her arms to make her warm. As he did, Harriet skittered past. He was glad Cat didn't see the animal, because right now he wasn't about to share her attention with anyone.

She shrugged. "A little." There was a slight change in her from the bold confidence she'd exhibited at the gazebo. She'd been quiet in the car, and now her mouth was drawn in a troubled line.

"I'll get us some towels," he said. If she had something to say, this would give her time to say it.

She held him back with a troubled look that stopped him in his tracks. "Wait, before we do this I—I need to tell you something."

His heart plummeted. "What is it?" He tried to sound

casual. *Please, God, don't let it be* this is wrong *or* I'm having second thoughts. *We've come too far.*

"It's—about Robert."

A bad sign. Bringing up the ex as they're about to make love. Very bad.

"What about Robert?"

"He said some things to me that I think you should know."

"Like what?" That gnawing feeling was back in his gut again. The feeling that made him want to strangle the son of a bitch.

A scarlet flush crept up her neck, and she kept gnawing on her lower lip. She looked so uncomfortable, he wanted to take her in his arms right there and tell her anything she had to say didn't matter, couldn't matter. Didn't she know that? "He said I—well, I had a problem when we—when we made love."

"A problem?" He raised a careful brow. On second thought, strangling was too kind.

"Yes. I wasn't ever able to…come. When I tried to talk to him about it, he said it was my problem, that he'd never had that issue with anyone else."

He smiled slow and predatory, wanting her to see how little anything that idiot said meant to him. Her eyes went wide with surprise. "Honey, the only thing wrong was that you were with that asshole." He ran his hands over her chilled arms. "Let me get you those towels."

He moved to go, but she held out a hand to stop him. "I have a better idea," she said. "You make us warm."

"I can do that." He wasted no time undoing his buttons and shrugging his wet shirt to the floor. Then he pushed her up against the wall and held her there, arms on either side of her head, his good knee fast between her legs, surrounding her with masculine heat.

He smiled as he slowly took in her dripping wet hair

and her streaked mascara. He traced a drop of water that had fallen from her hair down her cheek, reveling in the fact that, running makeup or not, she was hands down the most beautiful woman he'd ever seen. She was beautiful on the inside as well as out, and he would prove it to her, starting right now.

With a quick flick, he pushed the strap of her bridesmaid's gown over her bare shoulder and lowered his lips slowly to the fine curve between her shoulder and neck. He nuzzled there, dropping soft kisses on her wet skin until she shivered and tipped her head back against the wall to give him better access. "Let's get you out of these wet clothes," Preston said in a low voice.

She turned willingly around and lifted her hair so he could undo her zipper. He unzipped it slowly, relishing every glimpse of her finely arched back. The undone zipper gave him access to her bare skin, and he couldn't help slipping his hands under her dress and caressing her, circling her waist with his hands, tracing over the sweet curves of her hips. Finally, his hands wandered upward to slowly skim over her lacy bra, memorizing the feel and shape of her breasts while he kissed her shoulders and back.

She placed her hands against the wall. "I—I'm afraid I'm going to fall."

"I've got you tight," he said. "Where was I? Oh, yes, here." Still standing behind her, he unclasped her bra, which freed him to circle each breast with his hands. He rubbed slowly over her nipples until they grew taut under his touch and she squirmed, pushing her sweet ass against him until he thought he'd died and gone to heaven.

"They're small," she said.

"Beautiful," he said, devoting his attention to gently fingering each tip. With his teeth, he tugged down one side of her dress, then withdrew his hands from her body long enough to pull it and her bra off the rest of the way. Before she could turn around, he pulled her gently toward him so that her spectacular ass ground into his crotch. His hands roamed her body freely, memorizing her curves as he glided from her breasts to the edges of her lace panties, where he paused at the waistband for just a moment. "I love having you in my arms," he whispered in her ear. "I love the feel of you, your beautiful lines and curves. I've been dying to make love to you from the moment I saw you last fall at that wedding. After all this time, Cat, I can't believe you're really here." His fingers traced the waist of her lacy panties where they rested against her flat abdomen. He teased around one leg opening, lightly grazing her skin with his fingers until he heard her sweet gasp.

His arm encircled her, holding her tightly against him as he worked a finger under her panties. Her breath grew ragged, and he was thrilled at how she trembled under his touch. "Cat," he said softly, dropping kisses on the back of her neck.

"What is it?" she asked in a throaty whisper. He swept his fingers lightly around her feminine folds, loving that she was wet and slick for *him*. He continued to tease her until her head rolled back on his shoulder and she fought for equilibrium, her breath coming in soft sobs. "Oh God, what are you doing to me?"

"Making love to you." His fingers teased back and forth, homing in on her intimate core. "I was a fool not to make you mine before I left. I've regretted that every day of my life since."

He gave her shoulder a playful bite as he slipped his finger into her hot wetness. She quivered under his touch, arching her back against him. The feel of her soft, smooth skin against him made him crazy, but he focused on his task. "Enjoy it, sweetheart." Relentlessly, he added a second finger to the first and was thrilled when she moaned aloud, her body tensing.

"Preston—no—I—I need to see you. Don't want to come like this."

"Why not?" He nipped her earlobe playfully. "We have all night. I want to feel you come apart in my arms, baby. I want you to let go for me." Showing no mercy, he worked magic with his fingers, caressing a breast, rubbing a taut nipple as she clung helplessly to the wall. He loved every minute of it, loved how responsive she was, reveled in her soft whimpers and moans as she reacted to his touch.

At last her hips bucked against him, and she let go, crying his name into the dim room. He held her, drawing out her climax as long as he could, until she collapsed against him. When she turned around, she had tears in her eyes.

"You were saying something about some idiot?" he said, grinning, as he held her close, kissing her neck, taking in the sweet scent of her hair, the soft feel of her skin, trying to comprehend that she was here with him, really *here*. And nothing else mattered.

"It—that wasn't supposed to be about me."

"Honey, that was just an appetizer," he said, pulling back and looking into her eyes. "Wait till we get to dessert."

• • •

Cat's whole body felt shaky, like if she stopped holding on to him, she'd collapse into a boneless pile on the floor. She felt safe in his arms, secure, yet free at the same time, something she'd never felt with Robert, who'd do a play-by-play about their lovemaking and critique her every move.

Preston had made her come as easily as if it were brushing her teeth or riding her bike. He'd whispered things to her like how beautiful she was and how he loved touching her. The man was gentle, confident, and kind. Not to mention superhot.

She couldn't wait to do the same to him.

"If I didn't have this bum leg," he said, "I'd pick you up and carry you to the bedroom."

"Walking is nice," she said, wrapping herself around him and kissing him. "Healthy for you, too."

Preston took her hand and led her down a carpeted hallway. She followed him on wobbly legs. He stood in front of a big bed, covered with a neutral comforter and tons of down pillows, and began unfastening his belt. In the light of the single lamp on a bedside table, she saw the proud warrior in him, the dragon curling its tail down his left arm, his muscles flexing as he went through the motions of the everyday task. That's when it hit her.

He stopped and stood in front of her, cupping her face in his hands. "You're crying."

"I was thinking how lucky I am to have you here. What if I'd lost you? What if you wouldn't have come back?"

He pulled her into his arms and lay back on the bed, pulling her on top of him. The combination of the hard muscle and smooth skin of his chest against her breasts nearly undid her. "Don't," he said, looking at her with his intense blue eyes that were full of tenderness and desire. He wiped her tears and stroked the hair back from her face. "I made it back, safe and sound."

He said it like it had never occurred to him that someone would be so pained by his loss. "You'll never know the terror that went through me when I found out what happened to you," she said. "I wanted to be the one by your side. I wanted to be there for you. You don't have to shoulder all your burdens alone."

"I'm sorry, Cat. I'm sorry for shutting you out."

She worked on his belt buckle until finally he reached down and helped her undo it. He watched her—no, he *allowed* her to unzip his pants and pull them with his boxers down his legs, carefully navigating around his brace.

Although she did slow a bit admiring his cock, long and proud, and thought again what a beautiful man he was and how right it felt to be here with him.

She surprised him by starting at his calf, placing gentle kisses on the skin above his ankle, ignoring his protests. It was so like him not to want to be fussed over. "Now it's your turn, okay?"

And she'd better stop crying. It had to be enough that she had him now, that after all his pain and conflict, he was here. She wanted to give him everything, all of herself, but she knew how reluctant he was. She wouldn't demand more, but she would give him all she had.

He gave a wide grin. She reached up and pushed on his chest, forcing him to lie back and relax. She left a trail of kisses on his calf, fingered the Velcro-wrapped brace that caged in his scarred and battered knee. When she kissed his knee, he froze. "No, Cat, don't," he said.

She skirted the brace, knowing he didn't want her to see his knee. Honest, terrible words rose to her throat but she bit them back. Words he would never accept, like *I love every part of you. I always have, and I always will.* "I treasure every part of you," she said instead. "I'm so happy to be here with you. I've longed for this forever." She kissed his inner thigh, then moved over to his cock. Grasping his length, she ran her hand up and down his shaft until he groaned with pleasure.

"You don't have to—"

"Does this feel good?" She licked the tip, then put her mouth over him, taking in as much as she could until he gave a grunt of pleasure.

"I'll take that as a yes," she said, using her hand to slide up and down his length and alternating with her mouth.

He lay still, his eyes riveted on her every move. Then strong arms pulled her up, up, until she was lying on top of him, her hands on his perfect chest.

"That felt so damn good, but it's been way too long. I want to be inside you, Cat. Now." He pulled himself up and struggled to reach over to a nightstand drawer. She leaned over and opened it, taking out a condom. "Thanks," he said as he tore open the package and sheathed himself.

"My pleasure." She said it glibly, teasingly, but she felt anything but as she straddled him, poising her body over his.

He never stopped looking at her with an intensity that nearly brought tears back to her eyes, but he didn't speak. She wanted to tell him so many things. That she'd loved him for years, that she would do anything to stop his pain, that she'd dreamed of this very moment every night before she slept and every morning when she woke. But she didn't want to spook him, didn't want to pressure him to say more than he had. So she just decided to love him.

She bent low to kiss him, her hair falling around her face. He brushed it back, gazing deep into her eyes. "You're the reason I survived that hellhole," he said, cupping her face with his hands. "You made me laugh when there was nothing to laugh about. Thinking of you and how full of love and life you are made me want to stay alive and make it home. It's always been you, Cat."

She cried out his name as he filled her, her inner muscles taking his length, all of him as she trembled, as sensations and feelings overcame her and words and thoughts fled.

His kisses lit her on fire, stroke after deep stroke, his tongue possessing her mercilessly. His hands skimmed over her back and grabbed her ass as he moved his hips to their rhythm, and she clung to him, buried her face in his neck and held on while the waves of pleasure engulfed them.

They let loose together. As the world shattered around her, Cat clutched him hard, holding on to the hard smoothness of him, languishing in the soft warmth of his skin, his flesh-

and-blood *realness*, and vowing that come hell or high water, she would never let him go.

Preston rolled them on their sides, wincing just a little as he tried to keep the weight off his braced leg. He held her close, stroking her hair and murmuring sweet things to her. She curled into his chest, against the fierce dragon she once regarded as something that needed to be slain, but now seemed more protector and defender, part of him that would always keep her secure and safe.

She lay there reveling in the feel of his arms wrapped around her, the scent of his soap mingling with the unique scent that was him and only him. Nothing had ever felt so right. After a while, she reached up to kiss him softly on the cheek, but his eyes were closed and his breathing had deepened and slowed. He wore a peaceful expression in sleep that was so different from his usual hypervigilance while awake. She stretched out against him and thanked her lucky stars that he was hers at last.

She was almost asleep when she heard a little *thud* at the bottom of the bed. She opened her eyes to find the cat pawing its way up the comforter toward them. She reached out a hand to scratch behind its ears and encourage it to curl up in a ball next to her.

"Harriet, you look like you're right at home in this bed. I'll bet you sleep here every night. Preston's a big old softy, isn't he?"

"She's not talking, and neither am I," Preston murmured.

"I promise I won't tell a soul." Cat leaned back against Preston's firmly muscled chest, enjoying the warm feel of him and the light pressure of his hand as it rested on her hip.

"Except I don't think you should call me that," he said.

"What—a softy?"

In response, she felt the very *un*softness of his arousal at her back, and his arm dip down past her waist. "Maybe you should tell Harriet to go sleep somewhere else," Cat said.

"Why's that?" Preston asked.

She turned toward him. "Because I don't think any of us are going to get much sleep tonight."

· · ·

The room was still dark when Preston startled awake. He bolted upright in bed, his typical overactive response to any noise, especially one in the middle of the night. Rummaging through his bedside drawer, he felt around until he grasped the cool, hard handle of a knife. When the room suddenly flooded with light, he was leaning against the mattress brandishing it, his heart racing as he looked frantically around. As he stood upright, he stumbled, forgetting he'd taken off his brace after the last time they'd made love. A shooting stab of pain shot through his leg and made him buckle, but he caught himself on the side of the bed.

There was no time to focus on the pain. Cat, her hair disheveled from sleep, had a sheet wrapped around herself and was standing at the side of the bed. It took a minute for him to clear his head enough to hear what she was saying. Through the soothing tones he made out the word "phone."

Shit, his phone was ringing. He was leaning naked beside the bed holding a fucking knife because his damned phone was ringing. Emblazoned on his mind as he took the phone from Cat was the look on her face. It bespoke confusion, worry, and worst of all, fear. He'd made her afraid. All because he couldn't distinguish between a simple phone call and gunfire.

His hands trembled as he took the phone from her and answered it.

He shook his head and focused, finally comprehending the words. "Yes, thank you," he managed through a haze of discomfort. "I'll be there in about an hour."

He pressed the call end button and sat down on the bed, fumbling for his brace.

Cat stood next to him. "What is it?" she asked.

His fingers felt sluggish, like they were coated with oil. A curse flew past his lips, but it didn't bring comfort. "It's my brother," he said. "He—he's in the hospital. Alcohol poisoning."

"Alcohol poisoning? What does that mean?" Cat walked over to his dresser, pulled out jeans and a shirt for him.

"He passed out, and his buddies couldn't wake him up. So they took him to the hospital. He was celebrating his twenty-first birthday."

"Is he—is he all right?"

"He's getting a CT scan now because they're not sure if he hit his head when he passed out."

"I'll drive you."

He didn't want her to drive him, see the fault lines of his family exposed. It was bad enough he'd just held a knife out to her. "I'll call a driver. Go back to bed."

She was already putting on her own clothes. "I'll sit in the waiting area. You won't even know I'm there." She stepped over to him, her dress already on. "Please let me help in this small way."

It seemed his life was one crisis after another, and she was privy to all of it. He'd turned her away once, but she kept coming back. He'd sworn this time would be different, that he'd try to let her in. Still, it seemed he was always the one in need of help.

"You'd do the same for me." Her hand combed lightly through his hair, smoothing down the parts that were sticking up at odd angles from sleep and all their lovemaking. The simplest gesture. For a moment, he closed his eyes at the strange sensation of being cared for. Then he took her hand and flipped it over and kissed her palm. "I'm sorry about…

the knife. The phone startled me. To be honest, it doesn't take much."

"You always sleep with knives?"

"Habit."

She handed him his belt and smiled. "Any chance we can substitute that for something soft and harmless like maybe a second cat?"

Chapter Fifteen

Preston hated hospitals. Especially ERs. This ER was a flood of bright lights, beeping monitors, and murmured voices, all bringing back memories that were best forgotten. He forced himself to walk up to a desk. His bad leg was throbbing now, but he ignored everything to get to his brother. Cat was only parking the car, but her absence was palpable. For once, he didn't want to face this alone.

A nurse guided him back to a curtained room where his brother lay. Jared's youthful face was angelic in sleep, reminding him of all the times Preston had come in late at night from some job or another and headed back to check on him in his bed. He'd tried desperately to preserve that innocence and do everything in his power to keep Jared far away from their father's influence. He'd tried to teach his brother right from wrong.

These past few months he'd been so caught up with his own issues, he'd left his brother on autopilot. And this had happened.

"Everything's okay?" Preston asked the nurse, an edge

of worry in his voice. That was when he stopped cold. There, sitting at his brother's bedside, was his father. He was thin as always, like a rangy, beat-up coyote. For once, he didn't have a cigarette in his mouth, which Preston was certain was not his own choosing. His father turned his gaze on Preston, and in that instant, he was startlingly aware that they shared the same exact blue eyes.

"Hi, son," his father said.

Preston managed not to cringe. He didn't want to acknowledge the greeting but forced himself to respond with a nod. Fortunately, the nurse was talking, and he directed all his attention to her. "He's a lucky boy, because his friends brought him in when they couldn't wake him up. The doctor will be in to talk to you in a minute, so you can have a seat." She pulled up an extra chair she'd borrowed from the next room over.

Preston exhaled a pent-up breath. Jared was alive. He was okay. Oh hell, *was* he okay? What if he'd hit his head, broken bones, any of that? He stopped the nurse from leaving with his words. "Has he—been awake yet?"

"He was able to tell us his name, and he knew where he was. But he'll be resting for a while. We want to observe him until all the alcohol has left his system and he's alert and talking."

Relief nearly brought him to his one good knee. Preston thanked her and lowered himself into the chair to wait, wishing his father would do his usual disappearing act and wondering why the hell he hadn't. He texted Cat not to come back yet. There was no way he wanted her to see his father.

"So are you just going to give me the silent treatment?" his father asked. "I care about him, too."

Preston suppressed a snort. That same hostile tone. That same I'm-your-father-respect-me mentality. As far as Preston was concerned, their father had given up any entitlement to any moniker remotely meaning "parent."

Suddenly, Cat's face appeared in his mind as he'd seen her earlier that night, beautiful and relaxed and smiling. Cat, who took in straggly stray animals and men who were best passed over. Who opened her heart to children and thought the best of everyone. Maybe her influence could help him try to be forgiving. Or at least tolerate his father until he could get Jared the hell out of here. Maybe people could change if given enough love and a chance, but with his father, he wasn't betting the ranch on it.

"I'm not ignoring you." That was pretty polite, but he couldn't bring himself to call him "Dad." "I thought you were headed back to rehab." At least, he'd hoped he was, but frankly, it was no surprise that he didn't return.

"Listen, I wanted you to know I'm planning to move to Florida in a couple days. I'm staying with my girlfriend now, deciding my next step."

"Great. I hope it works for you this time."

Preston tuned him out. All he cared about was Jared. Making sure he was going to be okay. That he wasn't brain damaged or hadn't broken his neck or cracked his skull or anything else he didn't even know to ask about.

"How's the leg?" his father asked. Preston lifted his head, surprised his father had asked about his well-being, but not caring to make useless small talk. "Improving," he said, although the pain was pulsing like a car's subwoofers that are turned up way too loud at a red light.

His father snorted. "That's what they told me about my neck. But I hope it works out better for you."

Yeah, I do, too. His father had had more than a couple neck surgeries. His chronic pain issues had led to him becoming addicted to painkillers and self-medicating with alcohol.

"You know," his father said, "I was hopeful I could put my life together after the war. I had your mother, and you two boys were small."

Preston tried not to fidget his good leg. He didn't want to hear this. Didn't want to rehash the old, painful memories because he knew how the story ended, and it wasn't happy. "You went through some hard times," he said. "But you look better. I want you to know your therapy is covered. And anything else you need."

"Well, I appreciate that. You know, we were dealing with my surgeries and you kids being young. I loved your mother. She needed me to be strong for her. I wanted to be, but I just couldn't. I'm ashamed to say I lost it. I hid from the pain with alcohol. I wasn't a good husband."

Preston winced. That last stint in rehab, brief though it was, must have made him want to get all that stuff off his mind. Good for him, bad for Preston. "That's in the past, Dad. Those were tough times but we all survived, and you've got a new life now." That's as charitable as he could be. He just wanted his father to leave so he could sit with Jared until he woke up. But his father kept talking.

"What I'm trying to tell you, son, is you're lucky you're a ladies' man. Not tied down to one woman. You can get your shit together without having other responsibilities. Guthrie men don't do relationships well. We destroy the people we love. And it looks like all of us are cut from the same cloth." He tilted his head at Jared.

Preston stood so violently pain shot clear up his leg and all the way through his back. He bit back the word "no," gritted his teeth to prevent it from escaping.

"He made one mistake. He's just a kid."

"That's how it starts. None of us can stay away from danger—or alcohol. We have a craving for both. We're not meant to settle down. You didn't know your grandfather, but he was the same way. God help the women who love us."

"People   can   change,   Vernon."   Preston   was

hyperventilating. He tried to slow down his mind and his breathing, but nothing was helping.

"Son, I don't care how many millions you have. Blood is blood. You are who you are."

Preston had to squeeze his eyes shut to try to block out the words. He was sweating, and the room was starting to spin. Thank God the doctor walked in at that moment so he didn't have to respond.

"How is he, Doc?" Preston blurted to the woman in scrubs and a white coat.

"I'm Dr. Greenwood," she said with a smile, shaking Preston's and his father's hands. "He's going to be fine, Mr. Guthrie—and Mr. Guthrie," she said as she turned to Preston's father. Preston's father had the decency to look appropriately grateful.

"He was doing shots for his birthday," she said. "Way too many shots. His friends found him at the bottom of some stairs, passed out and clammy, vomiting and unable to wake up. Thank God they knew to bring him in. We tanked him up with fluids and gave him glucose intravenously. One of his friends said he might have hit his head when he passed out, plus they weren't sure if he fell down the stairs, so we got neck X-rays and a CT scan. Those were negative. We're going to keep him overnight. He should be waking up sometime over the next couple hours."

Preston nodded, but he'd only heard the translation: *Jared was going to be okay*. He'd done something stupid, but he'd live to get over it and tell the tale. Hopefully as a caution to others.

"Why don't you go home, Vernon?" Preston said. "I'll stay with him and take him home as soon as he's able."

Vernon got up and stretched. "Think I'll take you up on that, boy." He took out his wallet. "I'm a little short on cab fare. Can you…"

Preston had never been more eager to shove a couple twenties at him so he'd go away. He was about to hand them over, but at the last second he tightened his grip. "I need to tell you something," he said. "I'll pay for rehab anywhere in the country, and I honestly pray that you decide to return, but I will not continue to give you money to support your lifestyle. Is that clear?"

"Yeah." His father's hands closed around the bills, and he laughed. "Clear as mud." Chuckling, a sick, hollow cackle, he left out the door.

Preston collapsed into a chair, relieved his father had left. His stomach felt like it was the barrel of a washing machine, spinning around and around. He couldn't remember pain so bad it made him nauseated. There was nothing more he wanted than to sit with his brother until he woke up and thank every saint in heaven that his brother was going to be fine. But his father's words kept churning in his head.

Hopeful I could put my life together after the war. I wanted to be strong, but I just couldn't. We destroy the people we love.

There was not a Guthrie curse. Or a predestination for badness. Just because he shared blood with a man who had ruined his own life and his relationships with alcohol did not mean Preston was headed down the same path. Logically, Preston understood. He tried to summon Cat's practical tone, and that way she looked at him, without judgment, like he could do anything he put his mind to.

Then he looked at his achy, ugly leg. Would he ever run again? Do all the things he loved without hobbling along like a cripple? Be able to hold her in his arms and sail with her across a dance floor? Pick her up and carry her across a threshold? Not think that a ringing phone signaled a full-scale terrorist attack?

She had said it was all right not to carry all your burdens alone, but how long would she have to suffer with him? Was it ever fair to make someone do that? Maybe his father was right. It was better not to care for anyone, to get through your shit by yourself so you didn't drag anyone who cared down with you.

"Mr. Guthrie, are you all right?" Preston looked up to see the doctor, her hand on his shoulder and a worried look on her face. He hadn't heard her come in. "I just wanted to tell you we're going to move you to another room down the hall where you can spend the next couple of hours. I can't help but notice you don't look very well."

He straightened up. Scrubbed a hand over his face. "I—I'm fine." His problems could wait. He wasn't about to leave Jared's side. And Cat. How was he going to call Cat back here when he was like this?

"Are you sure?" she asked. "You look pale and sweaty. We don't want you passing out, too."

She was smiling. A kind doctor, one he might trust. He didn't want any of this to be about him, but she was right. He did feel about to pass out, and if that happened, it sure wouldn't do Jared any good. He blew out a big breath and caved. "I'm a vet with a chronic knee injury. I've been at a wedding all weekend, and I think I did something really bad to it."

"Let me have a look, all right?"

He nodded and undid his brace. As she examined his knee, Preston tipped his head back in the chair and glanced at the TV screen mounted high in the corner of the room, struggling not to focus on the pain. An action movie played, with guys running and jumping, bombs blowing up and vehicles catching on fire. He grabbed the bedside remote and turned the volume to mute. He had enough noise rolling around his brain. His dad might be long gone, but his voice had taken up living in Preston's head.

• • •

Cat felt the eyeballs staring before she saw her family talking among themselves in the corner as she walked into the lodge for the next morning's brunch and headed straight for the giant coffee dispenser. She envied Maddie and Nick, already on the way to the Greek islands for their honeymoon. The women of her family were waiting to pounce and get the scoop about her night. She wasn't certain what all she would tell.

Not that it hadn't been the greatest night of her life—up until that phone call. Preston and she had connected—finally, finally—and every moment with him had been intense and all-consuming and a zillion times better than she'd ever imagined it would be.

But. A warning bell jangled through her sense of well-being. Maybe it had started with the wild look in his eyes when the phone rang and he'd grabbed that knife. Or maybe it was his exhausted, dispassionate voice when he told her he'd called one of his drivers to take her home from the hospital. He'd wanted to stay with his brother, felt it was unfair to make her wait, and didn't want her driving back in the middle of the night after so little sleep. She felt fine, but he seemed awfully preoccupied about something, so she'd just gone with it. She knew how upset she'd be if something had happened to one of her sisters or her brother and didn't want to give him extra worry. But he'd seemed almost...disconnected, and that had started a tiny pebble of worry that was starting to snowball into a boulder.

She checked her phone to see if Preston had sent her an update on Jared's condition. Nothing. It had been difficult to wake up after so little sleep, but she had to make an appearance at breakfast or she would never live this down. She'd texted Preston as soon as she'd awakened, but no response.

He's just busy, she told herself. Still, that same feeling of unease had crept insidiously into her bones, a sense that after the spectacular night they'd had, something was off kilter.

It was probably just that she'd been burned before, by Robert and even by Preston himself. But things were different now, weren't they? They'd started to work things out. Even as she gave herself a pep talk, her grandmother's voice whispered in her ear, *you can't change people*. Cat herself had never had a suspicious nature, but she almost expected something to go wrong after her bad history with men.

She was suddenly surrounded by her sister and sister-in-law, both wearing Cheshire grins. "We want to know details," Jenna said.

"I have no idea what you're talking about," Cat said.

Liz got in her face. "Don't try to hide it. You've got that look."

"What look?"

"That look like you've been up all night being naughty," Jenna said.

"That look like you finally got some, and it was really, really good," Liz added. "Besides, we saw you two leave together last night looking very cozy."

"Let's sit down before Brady comes over here," Liz said, taking an anxious look around.

"Do you have a thing for him or something?" Jenna asked Liz.

"Of course not," Liz said, grabbing Cat by the elbow and steering her to a long table where family was gathered. "But when he knew he couldn't have you, he decided to try to hook up with *me*."

"Eww," Cat said.

"Don't worry. I can handle him. I was trying to be nice, but he's not getting the hint."

On the way to the table, Cat looked up to see Preston at

the door. Her face immediately heated just thinking of last night.

"Wow, you've got it bad," Liz said.

Cat shook her head. "No, it's just—just that—well, we got some things settled, and I feel really great about everything. And hopeful for the future." Yes, of course she did. What could possibly have changed from a few hours ago?

Preston approached and greeted her and the other women, then pulled Cat aside. Dark shadows circled his eyes, and stubble covered his face. His heavy brows were knit into a frown.

"How's your brother?" Cat asked.

"He's fine. He's at my place resting."

"Then why do you look so upset?" The tiredness wasn't what disturbed her. He had a wound-up tension about him. She could tell by his posture, the lines of strain in his face, and the way he fidgeted with the spoon in his coffee.

Preston sighed and looked at Cat. "My father was there. He never went back to rehab."

"Oh. Well, that could be a good thing, right? That he was there for your brother?"

"He's an angry, bitter man. Always spouting off about something. Everything's always more about him than anyone else."

Cat rested a hand on his arm. "It's a good thing Jared's got you instead."

Preston shrugged. "I hope so."

"Did your father…say anything that upset you?" Just a feeling she had that he was holding something back.

"Look, Cat, my father is always bad news. But he made me realize something. People with problems drag other people down. Relationships suffer. I've always known that. Hell, I grew up knowing that. I should know better than to make the same mistakes my father did."

"You're nothing like your father."

"How do you know that when *I* don't even know that?"

"Because I know." He drew away from her touch.

"Look, about last night…"

Oh God, no. Those were three words that could never lead to anything good. *Please don't. Not now.* Not when all of their family and friends were here. Not when she'd finally thought everything was perfect. "W-what about last night?"

"We—went kind of fast. Maybe we should—"

"Oh, hello, Preston," Cat's mom said. "Is everything all right? Cat said you had a family emergency."

"Thanks, Mrs. Kingston," Preston said. "Everything's fine."

"Can I bring you a plate, dear?"

"I'll go up in a minute, thanks."

"The wedding was so magical. You all looked so lovely."

"Speaking of wedding magic," Jenna said, pointing to Cat and Preston, "maybe you two will be the next couple to the altar."

Cat saw Preston stiffen. He put up his hands. "That's not going to happen," he said. His voice was low but Cat was sure at least Liz, who was on the other side of Preston, heard.

Preston must have seen something in Cat's face as she processed the comment he'd blurted out so quickly. He tried to backpedal. "I mean we—we're a long way off from that."

Cat's face flushed. Liz and Jenna shot her concerned looks. She tried to make light of it by flipping her hand in a careless wave. "Yeah, really guys, give us a break. I mean, c'mon, we just started dating."

Liz steered the conversation to another topic. Cat couldn't say which one due to the noise of all the blood whooshing through her ears. *Be reasonable*, she told herself. Of course he's going to be reluctant. After all, they'd just spent one night together. The best night of her life. Maybe it hadn't been like that for him.

"I'm going to get more coffee," she said as cheerily as she could. "Anyone else like some?"

As she walked away, her mind replayed what had happened last night. Everything had been so amazing. For the first time, she'd lost her inhibitions. Hadn't felt like she was acting out a script. Could that have possibly been all one-sided?

Preston met her at the coffee station. For the first time, she noticed he was walking slower than usual, and his limp was more pronounced. Dammit, she couldn't stop her hands from shaking as she poured another cup. He finally set the cup down himself and took up her hands.

His voice sounded soft and compassionate. She knew from the tone what was coming. "Cat, listen. I—this is too new. You can't expect me to want to shout it from the mountaintops right now. I need some time."

Suddenly off balance, Cat thrust her hand out behind her to grasp the table, tipping the coffee in the process. For a few seconds, she was mesmerized by the spreading stain as it engulfed the clean white linen.

She looked at Preston. He was unshaved, his hair rumpled. What the hell had happened in that hospital? Maybe under other circumstances she would simply let it pass. She'd understood and forgiven him for being too proud to share his pain with her, but she was done with acting like a doormat whose primary purpose was to please other people instead of herself.

"You need time?" she asked, forcing her voice to remain steady, even though she felt like she was going to hurl at any moment. Maybe he would explain this. Maybe it wasn't what she thought.

"I—I screwed up my knee somehow this weekend. The docs checked it out last night, and it looks like my surgery's got to get moved up pretty fast."

"Oh. You're upset about your leg and your brother. You've been up all night. I—"

"What I'm saying is I need some time by myself. I—I don't want to make a public announcement right now that we're together. I think it's best if—"

"Wait a minute. You took me home with you last night, and now you don't want to acknowledge what everyone already knows? You're ashamed that you slept with me? You couldn't be pushing me away again because that would be impossible."

Preston looked around. Her family was staring in their direction. "No—it's not like that. I—I had to take the pain medication after I got back from the ER. I didn't want to, but I had no choice."

"You were in that much pain, and you didn't even tell me?"

He shrugged. "I didn't want you to see me like that."

"Preston, my God, it's okay to take medicine when you need it." She waited until he finally made eye contact. "It doesn't mean you're going to become an addict like your father."

Suddenly, everything she'd been through with him over the past year welled up inside her. She'd ridden the roller-coaster ride for a long time and she thought that last night, she'd finally gotten off. She couldn't get back on again. She couldn't spend more time wondering if he cared about her. And she needed to tell him that right now. "All I've ever done from the moment I saw you at that wedding last September was love you. Yes, Preston, I love you, and I'm sure that's going to send you running even further away. If you plan to wait and solve all your problems and then come looking for me, I won't be here. I can't live my life waiting for you to love me back."

"Is everything all right here?" Derrick had stepped up to the coffee table. Behind him, her parents, grandmother, Liz, and Jenna were gathered with apprehensive looks on their faces.

"No, actually, Derrick, it's not," Cat said. Preston had the decency to look uncomfortable. "We lied to you. Turns out we're not dating after all. We were just trying to cover up that uncomfortable position you found us in last week. I'm sorry I lied."

Derrick's brows knit down, and he stared at Preston, but he didn't say anything. For now. Cat didn't really give him any time to respond, because she was on a roll, and she couldn't stop. "Grandmeel, I left that job interview in Charlotte last week. Do you know why? I hate being a journalist. I'm sorry, but I don't want to spend the rest of my life hunting down stories. I want to be a teacher. An underpaid, overworked, happy teacher. I'm going back to school, and I'll find a job to pay my way."

The concerned faces of her family stared at her, the crazy woman who was making a scene. Preston moved forward, but she put out her hand to stop him. "I'll be fine. You see, unlike you, I'm not afraid to lean on my family and friends. They may not like all my decisions, but I know they'll still love me in the end."

She got two steps away when she spun to face Preston again. "By the way," she said, "I really hope everything goes okay with your knee, but I think it's time you took my picture out of your wallet."

Cat walked out of the lodge and got halfway through the parking lot before she realized her car was in a hospital parking lot in Charlotte somewhere. Fortunately, Liz was behind her, holding up a car key. "This way, babe," she said, tipping her head over to where her own car was parked.

Cat managed to get into the car before the tears started leaking out. "Oh my God, I've made a scene. Thank God Nick and Maddie are long gone."

Liz put a hand on her shoulder. "It's okay. You finally told everyone exactly how you feel. Besides, Nick and Maddie are on their honeymoon. The last thing they're thinking about is us."

"I've ruined the breakfast. Everyone was happy. I should have kept my big mouth shut."

"Nah, I don't think it's completely ruined."

"Why not?"

"Once Derrick beats up on Preston, everyone will feel much better."

Chapter Sixteen

Lacey walked into Preston's office at Kingston Shoes and put a cup of coffee on his desk.

He looked up from his Monday morning paperwork. "You never bring me coffee." Derrick never laid a hand on him after the breakfast yesterday, but Preston must look pretty beat up anyway if Lacey was going out of her way to do things for him. Actually, he might feel better if Derrick *had* roughed him up. Anything was better than feeling his acute disappointment in their friendship.

"Yeah, well, I even made a pot myself. Let's just say I'm desperate for anything that will turn you back into a human being."

"What are you talking about?" He waved his hand over his desk full of paperwork. "I'm sitting here doing my job."

"You passed my desk without saying hi, you haven't said a word to anyone, and your shirt's on backward. Not to mention you look like you haven't slept for a week. Have you showered?"

"Of course I showered."

"Because your hair is sticking up." She licked two fingers then leaned over to smooth it down, and he backed away.

"Okay, enough already. Thanks for the coffee." Preston took a sip and made a face. "Except this stuff might just kill me instead of help me."

"Is there anything I can help with?"

He set the cup down. Misery swamped him. Hell, there wasn't anything anyone could do to get him out of the mess he created. He couldn't stop thinking about Cat. Couldn't stop hearing his father's words echoing in his ears. The drilling pain in his knee wasn't helping either, but at least it was more under control now. "Thanks, Lacey. But no. There's nothing."

"Well, I'm right here if you need anything, okay?" She gave him a concerned look before she began walking out.

"Wait."

She turned around. "Yes?"

Preston closed his eyes. This was hard, opening himself up to people. "This is our last day here, and I—I wanted to thank you for—for always doing your job. I know I'm not very expressive about things, especially these last few months, but I value your service. You're a great employee. Even if you do meddle in my personal life."

"I'm not sorry I told Cat, if that's what you're talking about. But thank you. I'll take that compliment under advisement the next time I ask for a raise."

She stood there, unmoving. He put his elbows on the desk and raked his hands through his hair. "I lost her, Lacey. I lost her for good." He didn't know why he said it. Usually he handled his pain by himself. Maybe he was sick of being an island. Or maybe his despair was just too great, and he could really use a friend.

"I'm sorry," she said gently. "Can I say something?"

"No, but I have a feeling you're going to do it anyway."

"You're one of the kindest men I've ever met. You gave

me this job and the opportunity to better myself. You paid for my mother's cancer consult at MD Anderson and made sure I wouldn't find out about it."

"But you did anyway?"

She grinned. "You're smart, but you can't hide much from me. Anyway, boss, you cut everyone slack…except for one person. Maybe it's time to give yourself a break."

Preston wished he could, but all he could think of was how hopeless his situation was. Surgery followed by more months of rehab. Of needing help. Of dealing with his own problems and head issues. Of feeling like he wasn't ever going to be a whole man again. How could he ask Cat to sign up to ride with him on his own personal journey to hell? "Thanks. I—I'm not exactly sure how to do that."

"Well, if it helps, Cat seems to love you just as you are. Crankiness and limp and all. You might not be able to find that anywhere else. Think about that, boss." He lifted a brow to warn her not to get too cheeky, but of course she ignored him. "Besides giving you my insightful advice, is there anything else I can do?"

"Well, there is one thing," he said, cracking a smile. "Promise you'll never make me coffee again. This stuff tastes worse than sewer water."

He heard her chuckle as she left the office. "Lacey," he called.

She stuck her head back in the doorway. "Yes, my liege. What is it?"

"I—I wanted to tell you you're a good friend." He cleared his throat. "And I appreciate your advice."

"It's damn good advice, too. You should take it," she said as she finally left.

God, it was hard being open and honest with people. He didn't really feel better but—well, it *was* good to have a friend.

Lacey hadn't been gone a minute when a knock on

the door made Preston look up. "May I come in?" Henry Kingston asked.

Preston moved to stand, an old habit from the military that had to do with respecting your seniors, but Henry shooed him back down. "No need to stand up for me, son. I thought we'd take a few minutes to talk business. Is now a good time?"

"Of course." Henry shut the door, an unusual move that made Preston's stomach churn worse than the coffee. He half expected Derrick to show up as well for a private roughing up.

"Look, Mr. Kingston, if this is about—"

The older man cut him off. "I know you're leaving today, and I wanted to make sure we're squared away on the new CEO. I also heard you're headed back to surgery and want to wish you the best." Preston couldn't even begin to wrap his head around the fact that this man was still talking to him after what he'd done to his daughter, but he forced himself to keep it professional.

"Thanks," he said, clearing his throat. Before the silence could get uncomfortable, he got to business. "I've reviewed the files on all the candidates," Preston said. "Brady's definitely the one that scores the highest on education, competence, and likability factors." Basically, he was a shoo-in. Preston squeezed the bridge of his nose and tossed the file to the desk. "But there's a concern I have."

"What is it?"

"He talks all the proper technical talk—metrics and units and markets and outsourcing work to China to increase productivity, but—"

"But what?"

"He has no heart for the mission of the company, sir. He's all about productivity and the bottom line. I'm sure he'd make the company a success on paper, but he doesn't seem to care about the tradition of the shoes, that they're American made, that many of the folks in town have been working here for two generations. My concern is that he'd sacrifice people for profit."

Henry sat back in his chair and laughed.

"Sir?" Preston raised a brow. Did he say anything funny?

"I knew I liked you, son. You just said what I came in here to say. This Brady guy looks perfect on paper, but he's going to send the company in a direction I've fought against all my life. I know every worker's name. Their families, too. Their kids and now even their grandkids. I want my company to be a place where people are proud to work. Where they're encouraged to be creative and contribute to the products and the good of the company, not be robots shuffled on an assembly line, doing the same task a zillion times a day."

"I can continue to screen résumés for you even after I leave town. I think broadening our search to people who are in management at more specialty-oriented manufacturing companies— " He scratched a few notes on a pad.

"I had a slightly different idea." Henry sat forward.

Preston looked up. Henry was eyeballing him calmly, his hands interlocked, slowly twiddling his thumbs. "Why don't you do it?" Henry asked.

"I beg your pardon?" His job was to match CEOs to the right companies, not run a company himself. He traveled all over, barely had a chance to enjoy his lake house, let alone be a part of a community. Hell, he'd never been part of any community.

"You understand the direction Maddie's going with her shoes, and how we also want to maintain our standard lines. You're going to be stationary for a while as you rehab your injury. Why don't you do the job?"

Preston put down the pen and stared at Cat's father. "Frankly, sir, after what's happened between me and your daughter, I'm not sure how you can make me such an offer."

"This doesn't have anything to do with Cat. It has to do with you."

Preston must have looked puzzled. He was completely floored. How could this man, who must surely want to kill him for hurting his daughter, be offering him the top job at his company? He was asking him to take a leadership role at a time when he thought of himself as anything but.

"I'm humbled, sir, but I don't deserve your consideration. I tried to push your daughter away after I got hurt, but she kept coming back and coming back until I just couldn't help myself. But I'm not the right guy for her."

"Care to explain that?"

"Men in my family don't handle long-term injury well."

His eyes narrowed. "Do you love my daughter?"

God, of course he did. But he would only poison her optimism and her belief in people. "That's a complicated question."

Henry laughed again. What was with this guy, anyway? He was sitting there as calmly as if they were having a chat about last night's ball game. "Can I show you something?" Henry asked.

Without waiting for a reply, Henry stood up and lifted his right pant leg to midcalf level. Preston craned his neck over the desk to see. At first, he saw nothing wrong. His sock over his calf. As he raised the pants, he saw the unquestionable cosmetic cover of a prosthesis. Preston looked up at Henry, whose eyes were the same bright green as Cat's.

"Grenada, 1983. I was just married at the time. I came back with more missing than my lower leg." He paused. "I know what you're dealing with, son. You feel like you're not going to be yourself again, but believe me, you will be. You'll rely on the strength of character deep inside you that made you go fight for your country in the first place, and if you're smart, you'll rely on the people who love you."

"With all respect, my father was a vet, too," Preston said. "His injury is what started all his problems. I don't want to drag your daughter down with me."

"You're nothing like your father. Even before he went to war, he may have lacked what I call a moral compass, but I'm not here to trash anyone. The point is, it doesn't matter what your father did or what his life's been like. You're an officer and a graduate of West Point, and you can use your mind and your reason to change the arc of your life. Just because you were born to that father doesn't mean you'll end up like him. You're your own man—you always have been, and you always will be."

"I'm sorry for hurting Cat."

"I'd say that to who needs to hear it. Go out there and be the man you were meant to be—someone who isn't ashamed to say he needs someone." Henry stood. "I came to say what I had to say, so I'll be going," he said.

Preston got up and dumbly shook Henry's hand. For once, words escaped him. Was it possible to escape a past you wanted no part of? To surmount problems that felt like they'd never go away? Maybe it was, if you wanted something more than anything you've ever wanted in your life.

He wanted to be whole, to have love. *To have Cat*, whom he loved with all his heart. He wasn't sure he could be the man she needed him to be. But maybe it was time to try.

"Think about things," Henry said with a wave as he left the office.

When the new driver Preston hired dropped him off at home, he was surprised to find his brother pacing the great room in his bare feet and texting on his phone, his hair still wet from a shower. Thank God Preston had gotten him out of the hospital before their father had an opportunity to get to him. "Glad you're up and about," Preston said, setting a bag of groceries down on the Carrara marble island in the kitchen. "How are you feeling?"

"Besides still having the headache of a lifetime, I'm okay. Listen, Pres, I—I need to get back to school. It's bad enough I stayed here an extra day. I'm trying to get one of my friends with a car to come pick me up."

Jared had finals coming up and Preston understood he wanted to get back. But he also understood he was embarrassed by what had happened and they hadn't talked much about it. Jared, still pacing, looked edgy and ready to bolt. "I can get you back to school," Preston said, "but I thought we'd have a meal together first. What do you say?"

"I really should go. I've got classes all day tomorrow, and I feel like I'm behind."

Preston walked over to his brother and put his hand on his shoulder. "Stay for dinner. It's been a long time since we had a talk. My driver can take you back right afterward. Please."

Something flickered in his brother's eyes. Preston had the sensation of looking in the mirror. Maybe his brother was just as in need of someone to reach out to him as Preston was. He wanted to reach him. Have a heart-to-heart. Make sure he knew he was loved even though he screwed up.

Jared broke into a sudden grin. "Depends on what's in the bag."

"Two sirloin steaks, baked potatoes, salad. Thought I'd toss the steaks on the grill."

"Dessert?"

"Ice cream."

"I'll stay."

They worked together to prepare the meal. Preston refrained from opening a beer, pulling out a couple of Cokes instead. They ate dinner on the patio, under the shade of some big oaks. A light breeze was blowing off the lake that made the spring evening pleasant.

"So tell me about your plans after graduation," Preston said. He'd gotten Jared to stay for dinner. Now to get him to talk.

Jared shrugged. He was playing with his Coke can, crushing it between his hands. "Don't worry. I turned in my grad school acceptance."

"Could you please sound a little more thrilled about that?" Preston asked, stretching out his bad leg near the fire pit.

"Grad school's important, and I'm going to be sure to make something of myself." The can crunched as he squeezed.

"I know you are. I'm not worried about that." Preston took a sip of Coke, trying to figure out just the right thing to say but not having a clue. What would Cat do? Meet the problem head-on, that's what. "Jared, it's okay if you don't want to become a psychologist."

His brother went quiet. He spent a long time looking into the fire pit. And mutilating the can.

"I really like psych," Jared said. "I'm just not sure I want to listen to people's problems all day."

"That's fair."

Jared jerked his head up. "What did you say?"

"I said, that's fair. What's your alternate plan?"

More silence, like he was getting up his courage. "Look," Preston finally said. "You shouldn't feel bad telling me how you really feel. I want you to do something you're excited about. Something that makes you happy."

Jared tossed the crushed Coke can onto his plate. When Jared glanced at him over the fire pit, Preston was reminded of when his brother was a young boy, always so worshipping. Now he worried that his brother wanted to please him a little too much, at the expense of his own happiness. Like Cat with her family. "You know that high school volleyball team I helped coach this semester?" Jared said. "They want me to be a real assistant coach next year."

"That's great." He could see how his brother's eyes lit up when he talked about coaching. Like it made him…happy.

"I like working with kids. And I love sports."

"So what are you thinking?"

"Maybe I'd like to be a high school counselor. Work with kids, you know? And a coach."

Preston stretched out his other leg and crossed his arms. "I can actually see you doing that."

"I applied to the wrong graduate program."

"An easy fix."

"No, it's not."

"Well, you can always try to apply somewhere that's not filled. Or worst-case scenario, work a year and apply again. Either way, you'll figure it out."

They sat watching the fire, listening to it crackle. Felt the soft spring breeze as it carried scents of fresh lake air and growing things.

"So if you need a job while you're figuring this out…"

"Yeah?"

"I might have a lead on something here in Buckleberry." He was pretty sure he could get Henry Kingston to give him a job as he'd done for Preston many years ago. "You interested?"

"Sure. Except that Dad's here."

And then there was that. "He showed up at the hospital, did you know that? He's on his way to Florida." He didn't want to hide things anymore from his brother. "To be honest, I think it was more because he wanted money from me than anything else."

"I don't want to have anything to do with him," Jared said. He poked a stick into the fire for a minute before he said, "I'm sorry I acted stupid and ended up in the hospital. I guess it's in the genes."

Preston frowned and sat up. "What are you talking about?"

"You turned out okay. But you've always known what you wanted. Look at me, ready to graduate, and I'm not even sure about my next step. I'm fucking up, just like him."

Preston reached over and grabbed his brother's arm. "Look at me, Jared. Don't ever compare yourself to our father. You couldn't be more different."

He could tell from his brother's eyes that he wasn't buying that. Worse, his brother actually thought *he* had it all together. "Look, your whole future is ahead of you, and it's going to be great. I don't think I've told you this enough, but I'm so proud of you."

"Yeah, I made you real proud, huh? You had to come to my rescue just like you do our old man."

"Everyone makes mistakes. The key is to learn from them and don't let them define you. That's the difference between us and him. Our father is who he is, and we can't help that. But we can be who we want to be—and don't let him convince you otherwise."

Preston heard the words come out of his own mouth. The very thought that Jared was anything like their father was ridiculous. He was as certain of it as he was his own name. And that's when it hit him. *He wasn't either.*

"I'm sorry I fucked up," his brother said. "You've done everything for me, and I didn't make you proud."

Preston placed a hand on his brother's shoulder. He remembered when that shoulder was bony and thin, when he was just a gangly teen, but he'd filled out a lot in the last year or two and was looking more and more like a man. "Somebody wise told me the best way to have a relationship is to share things. Not just the good, but the bad, too. I haven't shared much with you since I've been back from overseas. I was protecting you from things I didn't feel you should have to worry about. I thought I could shoulder it all on my own. I was wrong." He'd been wrong about so many things. He'd fucked up, too, big-time. How could he preach to his brother that everything was going to be all right, that he would work it out, without taking the same advice himself?

"I wish you would talk to me about what's going on with you."

"I supposed I felt like it was my job to shield you from all the ugliness we experienced growing up. You've had enough of that to last a lifetime. I didn't want you to have to deal with my problems, too."

"I'm not a kid anymore, Preston."

"No, you're not."

He drew his brother into a tight hug. He'd always had faith and pride in his brother. Just as Cat had always believed in him, imperfect, messed-up him.

"I love you, kid. After dessert, we'll hit the road, and I'll tell you what I've been doing the last couple months. Deal?"

Jared was nothing like their old man, and Preston wasn't either. He thought he wasn't whole because of his leg, because of the war, but the truth was, he wasn't whole without *her*. She was greater than all his imperfections. All he wanted was to humbly love her, it she'd allow it.

Preston hugged his brother again and slapped him a few times on the back for good measure before they brought out the ice cream. He knew his brother would learn from this mistake, just as he could learn from his. The next step was getting Cat to see that, too.

Chapter Seventeen

Cat's class had gone AWOL. They were nowhere to be found. She turned around and took the craft box from Grandmeel, who had offered to be her assistant for the afternoon, and set it down on the teacher's desk. "One of the other teachers walked them back from lunch. I wonder if she thought they had music or something?"

Grandmeel's gaze was darting everywhere, from the hanging flowers to the colorful bulletin boards to the giant tree painted on the wall with children's pictures hanging from leaves, trying to get a grip on everything. "How about I start setting up for the craft, and you go find them?" she suggested.

Cat glanced at the wall clock. "It's ten after, so I guess I better." Grandmeel walked into the carpeted story corner and started thumbing through picture books. "I remember reading all of these to you. Remember this one?" She held up *Strega Nona*.

"Remember when Mom and Dad came in to read to my class, and Dad dressed up like Strega Nona and brought the spaghetti pot?"

"I stood in the back of the classroom and took a video of it. We can watch it tonight." Grandmeel closed the book and walked over to Cat. "Listen, dear, I know you're having a rough time of it. I just want to tell you that after watching you this morning, I do believe you'll make a great teacher."

Well, what a surprise. A compliment from her grandmother. Genuine, too. "Thank you, Grandmeel."

"I suppose I always saw a bit of me in you. You do remind me so much of how I was as a young woman. My dream was always to be a journalist. Maybe I was somehow trying to live out that dream through you."

Her grandmother riffled through the box, suddenly very busy sorting different colored sheets of paper. Cat went up and put a hand on her arm until she looked up. "You didn't make me go to school for journalism. I chose that myself. I knew my heart wasn't in it, but I didn't have the courage to change course."

Grandmeel patted her hand. "You're a brave woman, Catherine. I know you'll be a success at whatever you do."

Cat gave her grandmother a squeeze. "Thanks, Grandmeel. You know, it's not too late. Buzz at the *Buckleberry Gazette* is looking for a human-interest reporter. That could be fun, getting the scoop on all the good gossip."

"I'll take that under advisement." She went back to sorting construction paper by color. "By the way, Eleanor Covington's son is coming back to town in a few weeks. Maybe…"

Cat smiled politely and headed to the door, pretty much drowning out the rest of the matchmaking plans. She wasn't ready to be fixed up with anybody. She was sad and lonesome and disappointed that Preston had shut her out again. For the first time, though, she felt stronger than she had in a long while. She'd managed to survive the weekend and even make it to work today. Even more than that, she knew more of who she was and what she wanted. Her life would carry on, even if it had to be without Preston. She would never regret putting herself out there and taking the risk for him, even if he couldn't love her back.

Just then a few lone guitar notes sounded from outside. They morphed into an unmistakable riff that Cat would recognize anywhere. Suddenly young children started clapping along to a beat and singing, their voices unmistakable. "Cather-ine, oh, baby! We like you. Yeah, yeah, yeah, yeah."

Giggles floated through the window. The chorus of children's voices was joined by another voice, loud and low and clear. A voice she would recognize anywhere.

The beat of her heart nearly drowned out the music. Adrenaline froze her to the floor. Grandmeel exchanged an incredulous glance. "Good Lord," she said. "Is that the tune to 'Louie Louie'?"

A grin broke out from ear to ear. "Yes, but those certainly aren't the words."

"Does anyone really know the words to that song?" Grandmeel asked.

They both ran to the row of windows that were tilted open to the bright spring day. In the schoolyard stood Cat's class, rowdy and laughing, singing along to the tune that Preston played on his guitar. In the background, her parents and sister stood smiling and waving.

Grandmeel turned to her and smiled. Cat could swear her eyes were a little teary. "Well, what are you waiting for?" Grandmeel said. "Go outside and claim your destiny."

"Thank you, Grandmeel." Cat gave her grandmother a kiss and headed out the door, where the kids swarmed all over her and led her to where Preston stood, his guitar slung over one of his big, sexy shoulders.

Preston took her hand and led her to the edge of the crowd, then dropped his voice low. "Catherine, I'm here to say I'm sorry. I can only offer you myself as I am and pray that that's good enough. You make me want to be the best version of myself. To be the man I was meant to be. With you by my side, I'll try every day to do that if you can forgive me." He turned around and shouted, "Okay, kids, hold up the signs."

Four kids in the front row brandished poster board signs, each containing a word scrawled in Magic Marker.

Cat felt a tug on her sleeve. "I can read that," a little girl named Angela said.

"Okay," Cat said, bending down. "Tell us what it says."

"It says, 'I—love—you—Cat.'"

"Thank you, sweetie," Cat told the little girl. The signs were blurring. Everything was blurring. She was smiling and crying, and she was worried she was upsetting the kids but she could not stop.

She felt an arm slip around her waist, and Preston whispered in her ear, "What it should really say is, I'm proud and stubborn, I hate asking for help, and I don't know what the future holds, but you're the best thing that's ever happened to me, and I'd be a fool to let you go. I love you, Cat. I only hope you can forgive me for being such an ass."

Then he kissed her. It was a soft, good kiss, the kind a man gives a woman he truly loves, when he holds her in his big strong arms and kisses her like they have all the time in the world to share many more. The kind of kiss he made himself keep to PG-level for a bunch of little kids but that held the promise of a lot more heated ones later when they were alone. In private.

Titters erupted from the kids.

"Hey, I thought we had to keep our hands to ourselves!" Tommy said, busting them.

Preston stopped kissing Cat long enough to ruffle the little boy's hair. Then Preston turned to Cat and shrugged. "Can't blame a guy for wanting to steal a kiss."

"It's okay to break the rules this one time," Cat said to Tommy. And to Preston, "You are a great kisser. And I love you, too."

Preston pulled out his phone and held it at arm's length, gathering her close. "Say cheese."

"What's this for?"

"New selfie for the wallet."

"I'm overwhelmed." And she really was all choked up.

"Okay, kids," Finn called from in front of the crowd. "Everyone follow me until Ms. Kingston is done having a smooch with her boyfriend," As she passed by with all the kindergartners in line behind her, she said in a low voice, "This was cute, but it's time to wrap it up and go in and take care of these little holy terrors."

"Just last week you called them little doe-eyed angels," Cat reminded her.

"It's almost the end of the school year. I'm getting tired."

"It's okay to drop them off with Grandmeel. She can handle them for another five minutes till I come in," Cat said.

"I'm telling you, these new substitutes are so demanding," Finn said to no one in particular. "Please don't be too long. Your grandmother can create a lot of damage to young minds in five minutes."

Liz came up from the crowd and hugged her sister, wiping away a few tears herself.

"Why, Liz, you really are sentimental after all," Preston said.

She poked him in the shirt. "I meant what I said. You hurt my sister, and I'll make sure you never walk again."

"Understood. Thanks, Liz."

"Don't mention it." She glanced at her watch. "Gotta go, I'm late for my one o'clock patient."

Henry and Rosalyn Kingston walked up with Derrick. "That was quite a performance, son," Henry said.

"Thank you, sir."

"I hope you'll consider my offer," Henry said.

"What offer?" Cat asked.

"You dad asked if I wanted the CEO position."

"Maybe you should take it. You did a terrible job finding the company a match. Come to think of it, you did a terrible job finding *me* a match, too."

"Hey, third time's a charm. There's only one man up to the job of being your boyfriend. And it's me." He turned to Henry. "I'd be honored, sir, to serve the company until we find the *right* person for the job. And I'll make it my top priority to find that exact right person. Except for now, I've had to turn the search over to my assistant. My surgery's scheduled for the day after tomorrow."

"I was going to tell you we want you to come for dinner later this week," Rosalyn said. "But maybe I can bring some real food to the hospital if you're up for it."

"Thanks, Rosalyn." Preston kissed her on the cheek.

"Thanks, Mom," Cat said.

"We're proud of you, son," Henry said.

Derrick walked up to Preston and shook his hand, then pulled him in for a hug. "Good thing you two are official now," he said. "I mean, this *is* real, right?"

"It's real," Cat said.

"Well, congratulations, and it's about time." He turned to Preston. "But Guthrie, remember. I can always call in the rain check for messing up that pretty face of yours if you ever hurt my sister again."

"I love your sister," Preston said. "I promise to do right by her this time."

"Thanks, Derrick. I think," Cat said, hugging her brother.

As they walked off, Preston turned to Cat. "I'm sorry we have to start off with me going into the hospital."

She slid an arm around his back as they walked. "I think

it's a little ironic. I mean, not everyone gets a chance to start all over again and do it right."

"It's going to be a full-time job, rehabbing this time, but I want you to know that I'm also going to consider it a full-time job trying to deserve you."

"I'll do the same right back," she said, tearing up again.

"I brought you a little something." He walked over to where his guitar case sat on the ground and picked up a large square white box, one of several, which he handed to Cat.

"What is it?" she asked as she dug into the pretty flowered wrappings. She pulled out the rooster lamp from the antique shop, that haughty, bright-colored crower.

"Wow. Spectacular."

"He works and everything." Preston pulled a lightbulb out of the box and held it up just to demonstrate.

"I love him, but where on earth are we going to put him?"

He shrugged. "I think he'd look good in the great room. With his partner to keep him in line, of course."

"You bought me the chicken, too?"

"Of course. They're a pair. He's going to remind you to stand proud and be amazing and to ruffle some feathers once in a while like you did mine."

"And what's the chicken going to do?"

"She's going to keep him in line when he gets too crazy. And remind him that he can't go it alone. That it's good to have company on the journey." Preston stepped closer. "Are you crying over poultry?"

"What's in the third box?" she asked, daubing at her eyes.

"Maddie and Nick's wedding gift was a little late in arriving. Want to see it?"

She peeked in that box, too. "It's the Louis XIV candlesticks."

"Um, they are Louis XIV candlesticks, but not the ones from the antique store."

She stopped touching them, afraid of how expensive they were. "So you raided the Louvre after all."

"Not exactly. I have good sources." He pulled some folded papers out of his breast pocket. "I have one more surprise. This is something just for us."

"Please tell me it involves private time and happens as soon as I get off work."

He laughed. "Close your eyes." He waited until she did, and even made her hold out her hands before she could open them.

"Oh my God," she said as she read the print on the two pieces of paper in her hands. "We're going to Hawaii. As soon as school's out."

"My doctor is setting me up with a whole rehab team over there. You may have to take in some tourist sites by yourself this time, though."

Cat put her hands on his chest, over his heart. "I have a better idea."

"What's that?"

"Let's save Hawaii until after the rehab. I'd be just as content turning on the chicken lamps and sitting outside enjoying the lake with you and our cat on your patio."

"It is a great view out there." But he was looking at her.

"I love you, Preston Guthrie."

"And I love you, Cat Kingston." He collected his guitar, but she enlisted some kids to help take that and the boxes to her classroom. He said good-bye to the kids and then to her at the door.

"Say, I'm going over to the coffee shop for a while. Will you pick me up when you're done with work?"

"You bet I'll pick you up. And I'm taking you straight home."

"A chauffeur after my own heart. Just what I love."

Epilogue

One year later

"School's out for summer," Preston said, holding out a bouquet of flowers at the door to Cat's classroom where she'd just finished a semester of student teaching. "What are your plans?"

She took the flowers, exclaiming how beautiful they were, and brought them to her nose to sniff. "Oh, hang out with my boyfriend at his lake house. Cheer him on at the Kingston Shoes Annual 5K tomorrow morning."

"That's boring. Let's do something a little different this summer." He stood in front of her with something behind his back. "Close your eyes." He tried his best to act casual, but his heart was racing like a Derby horse.

"What, no guitars this year? No choruses of children singing their versions of rock classics? No relatives hiding behind the door?"

"Not this year. Just a simple box."

Her eyes instantly teared up. "Oh, Preston."

He was quick to say, "It's not what you think. Open it."

She opened it to find a tiny ceramic box, with a tiny hinge.

On top of the box sat a rooster, a chicken, and three baby chicks. She opened it to find a diamond ring. He didn't think she saw much of the special ring he'd had custom-made just for her because her eyes had completely misted over, and her mouth dropped open in shock.

Preston dropped to his knee. Okay, it was his good knee, but his not-so-good knee was working pretty darn well after a year of intensive rehab. "I'll love you forever. Marry me, Cat."

She bent to touch his face and look into his eyes. "Yes," she said without hesitation, jumping into his arms until they both almost toppled over onto the floor. "How soon?"

"Now. Tomorrow. As soon as we can."

"That sounds wonderful." And then, both of them still kneeling, he kissed her. But this time, he didn't have to keep it PG, because no little kids were watching. After a while, Cat helped him up. He helped gather up her stuff, then she flipped the light switches next to the door.

"All ready?" he asked.

"All ready," she answered. Then he swooped her up and carried her out of the classroom.

"Congratulations on completing your student teaching," Preston said. "You've worked hard this year."

"Yeah, and so have you," she said, holding on with an arm around his shoulder. He never would have been able to support her weight a year ago. He'd barely been able to hold himself up then. He'd come a long way mentally, too.

"You've been with me all the way," he said.

She giggled. "You're supposed to carry me over the threshold on the way *in*."

"I'm practicing. So I get it right. I'd like to go and practice some other things, too, if that's all right."

"Take me home," she said, reaching out and closing the door quietly behind them. And before he did, he kissed the woman he loved again.

About the Author

Miranda Liasson loves to write stories about courageous but flawed characters who find love despite themselves, because there's nothing like a great love story. And if there are a few laughs along the way, even better! She won the 2013 Romance Writers of America Golden Heart Award for Series Romance and also writes contemporary romance for Montlake Publishing. She lives in the Midwest with her husband, three kids, and office mate Posey, a rescued cat with attitude. Miranda loves to hear from readers! Find her at mirandaliasson.com or Facebook.com/MirandaLiassonAuthor or on Twitter @ mirandaliasson.

Also by Miranda Liasson...

HEART AND SOLE

Maddie Kingston just walked away from everything in order to take over her family's struggling shoe business. Unfortunately, the majority of the company's shares have been bought out by none other than Maddie's ex-boyfriend, billionaire Nick Holter. Now Maddie needs his help, even if even if it means buying Nick from a charity bachelor auction. Between their families' feud and their own unfinished business, tempers—and emotions—run hot. *Too* hot. Because kissing with the enemy is a guaranteed shoe-in for trouble...

Discover more category romance titles from Entangled Indulgence...

THE MILLIONAIRE MAKEOVER
a *Bachelor Auction* novel by Naima Simone

Niall Hunter never imagined his penance for one hot-as-hell night with his best friend's little sister, Khloe Richardson, would be transforming her from a shy wallflower to a sultry siren. Helping her attract another man is torture. But Niall can't stop wanting her. Can't stop touching her. Can't stop, period. And damn if he can remember why he has to...

CAN'T RESIST A COWBOY
a *Paint River Ranch* novel by Elizabeth Otto

Carrie Lynn Waite has never known a time when she didn't love Levi Haywood. They were childhood sweethearts, but because of her illness, she was forced to move to the city, away from the ranching life. Now Carrie's come home only to learn her family's ranch is in trouble and Levi is back from the Marines, along with an undeniable attraction she can't resist. But some things never change. Now Carrie must decide between her future...and the cowboy she could never resist.

HIS HEART'S REVENGE
a *49th Floor* novel by Jenny Holiday

A CEO in his own right, Cary Bell is competing for a major client with his boyhood crush. He's never forgiven himself for betraying Alex Evangalista. But with his professional reputation on the line, he's going to have to find his inner cutthroat if he wants his new company to succeed. Alex isn't about to let his nemesis steal a client out from under him. It's time to break Cary's company—and his heart.

9 781533 111371